Waste Ground

Marc Ruvolo

SLASHIC HORROR
PRESS

ISBN-13: 978-0-9756380-9-5

Edited by David-Jack Fletcher

Interior Design by David-Jack Fletcher

Cover design by Christy Aldridge of Grim Poppy Designs

Praise for Waste Ground

"*Waste Ground* is a cosmic nightmare of fraying relationships and dogged determination converging in the mouth of a bizarre cult and the otherworldly entity they worship. Ruvolo keeps the action nonstop as he viscerally displays Portland's underbelly and the unseen hunger beneath our feet."
– J.A.W. McCarthy, Bram Stoker Award and Shirley Jackson Award finalist, author of SLEEP ALONE

"Fast paced and twisted, *Waste Ground* is a Venus flytrap that will inevitably capture you. Ruvolo's clever prose will keep you turning the pages of this cosmic story of cults and revenge until you have devoured it whole."
– J.V. Gachs, author of EPIPHANY

"Ruvolo expertly weaves a captivating plot with beautiful prose in a way few others can. Waste Ground is so much more than a terrifying and mysterious trip into a murderous cult, it's also a sad and deeply human story. The people and circumstances we fall into, are born into, and stay with because of fear, convenience, comfort, or all of the above, haunt this book. And the haunting is devastating. Waste Ground is visceral, frightening, and moving."

– Jessica Leonard, Author of ANTIOCH and CONJURING THE WITCH

"The novella is non-stop action, fast-paced, with good characterization and some insightful introspective moments on feeling unable to get yourself out of a rut. People (junkies, cops, vagrants, not in that order and certainly not all of sound mind) come and go with Portland in the background. The atmosphere is bleak and sad, though there are a few occasions that made me smile, smirk, or snicker."

– Milt Theo, Goodreads Reviewer

"This is a fast paced and really horrific cosmic horror novella. You never know if any of the characters are going to live. They face dangers of the human variety along with this THING in the ground which wants it's sacrifices cooked...and the cult members who are more than willing to do that even as their addictions creep up on them."

Other titles by Marc Ruvolo

Pieties

Sloe

Creep & Crow

Trigger warning: this book contains some sexual assault.

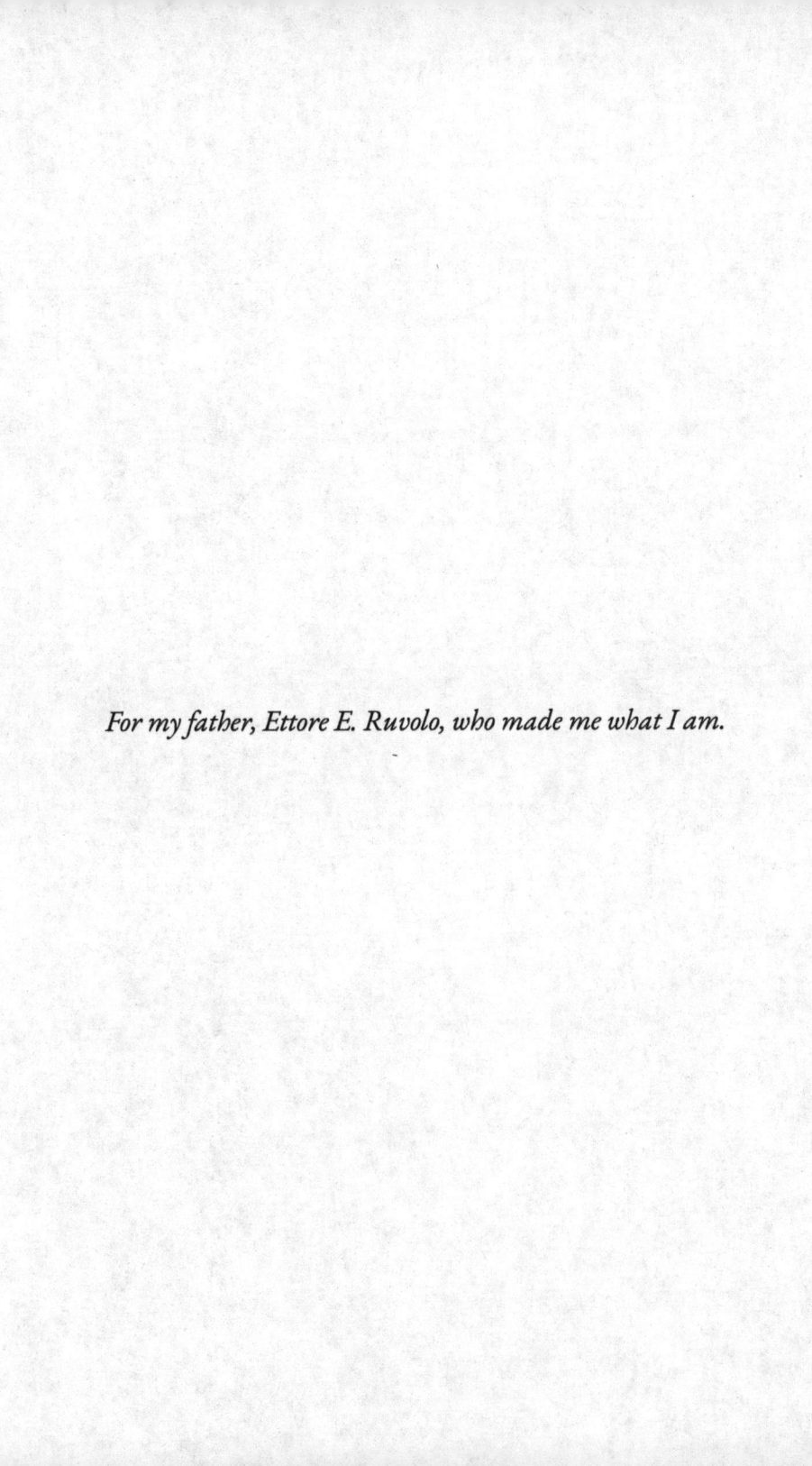

For my father, Ettore E. Ruvolo, who made me what I am.

PROLOGUE

DOROTHEA JERKS AWAKE.

A metallic rattling, like…the snare drums of a marching band, or hurricane winds banging the shutters. "Oh, what the fuck," she moans. "Uhhh, my head. Quit it, bitches. Errol? Errol, where the fuck are you?"

A rhythmic, relentless pounding:

…*ratatatatatatatatatatat…ratatatatatatatatatat…*

Bright lights blind her—car headlights, she slowly realizes—the noise echoing all around. Her eyes adjust, and silhouettes of people swim into focus. A large group, standing atop the cars, using sticks to hammer on the hoods like some apocalyptic drum circle. It's night, but there's no moon, no stars, and she's outside somewhere, ass in the dirt. Her hands are tied securely behind her back, a zip tie digging deep into her wrists. Panic sets in as the strange creatures

1

dance among the wheelless, gutted hulks, ruined cars painted with elaborate layers of cryptic graffiti.

"Errol!"

The last thing Dorothea remembers is driving with Errol to a party to buy meth, both already half in the bag. On the way, they stopped at Taco Bell. At the house party, their connection insisted on conducting business in an empty swimming pool, money was exchanged, then someone—*Errol? It's hazy*—handed her an open bottle of beer...and things had...*tilted?* Blurred to black. She'd been roofied, that much is clear. But how in hell did she end up here, and what the fuck is going on?

She squints into the glare, trying to blink away a head full of rolling fog. "Errol? Are you there? Errol!"

Something stirs beside her. "Hah. Where you from, kid?"

"Wha? Who's that?"

A face swims into view. A grizzled old man with a scraggly beard and bloodshot eyes, tiny, blurred stars tattooed on his weathered cheek. And Lord, he *stinks*. A smell noxious enough to pucker her dried-out mouth.

"Not Errol, haha. I said, where ya from? Here? Portland? Somewheres else?" His craggy voice sounds like it's been scraped from the bottom of a full ashtray.

"Uh." The world lurches around her. *Who is this person?* She strains to break the zip tie. "W-where the fuck are we? What's going on? What are those lights, and the—the *banging*?"

The old man sniffs. "The Kolchaks wanna look at all the tributes. They'll be turning off them lights when the ceremony starts. Won't need 'em when the flames blaze up high and hot." He coughs, a painful, congested sound from deep inside his chest, and she realizes his hands are bound, too.

"Tributes?"

Another man is lying to her right. He's slumped over, reeking of old piss, a crushed Coors can in his lap. And then she sees there are more, a whole line of people bound and sitting on the wet, trash-strewn ground. "Shit. Did you say *ceremony*?"

The cacophonous drumming stops. Someone howls—a low, mournful sound—and one by one, whomever it is out there joins in feral chorus. Dorothea struggles to rise, the zip tie digging into the bruised skin of her wrists, cutting the circulation to her fingers. "I gotta—I gotta, gotta get the fuck outta here."

"Easy girl," the old man says. "You ain't going nowhere. Not yet at least. Settle down and enjoy the show."

A woman wearing a spray-painted bike helmet and heavy boots passes through the wall of shifting light. She's carrying an old car tire. Pushing Dorothea back down, she hangs the tire around her neck. It's heavy, and stinks of rubber and gasoline. The woman upends a red can and a fresh stream of gas splashes onto the tire. Dorothea sputters, choked by the strong fumes, her brain whirring, dizzy and nauseous.

"Why—why are you doing this?" The gasoline pools in the dirt around her scuffed-up Nikes.

"Rejoice, brothers and sisters," the woman says dousing the unconscious man next to Dorothea. She's almost emptied the gas can before she continues. "Soon this sad, worldly life will be nothing but a memory. You're all food for Paradise! The crying is done! Now is the time for our joyous celebration! A new age is upon us!"

A skeletal, thin teenager with a mangy head of green hair hangs a dripping tire from the crazy old man's neck. "I'm food for Paradise!" the old man crows, laughing. "Hallelujah! Send me to Heaven well done!"

The car headlights fade, spots swimming before Dorothea's eyes. But it doesn't remain dark. First, she sees sparks, then flames, as hungry fire is passed hand to hand in the twisted steel henge of derelict cars. Before long, a dozen flickering torches creep toward the line of captives.

Dorothea struggles to break the zip tie. "What are you doing? Help! Someone help me! Errol! *Errol!* Where the fuck are you?"

The first man set ablaze wears an oversized three-percenter T-shirt but is naked from the waist down. He shrieks, writhing against his bonds, legs spasming and cock swinging as orange-and-blue flames engulf his body. Dorothea gags at the stink of cooked human meat. A woman with a drawn, foxy face and skin lesions of a long-term meth addict is next, her mouth pushed wide in a silent scream as the gasoline explodes to life, crisping her stringy hair. Three more captives go up in quick succession, their nightmarish howling cut short by the roaring intensity of the accelerant-fueled conflagration.

Fear and adrenaline drive Dorothea to her feet. Shrugging, she wrenches her arms left, and the heavy tire falls from her neck.

"Don't be foolish, girl," the old man growls. "This is an honor. And you'll never get away."

Dorothea makes it to the nearest car before a jiggling, sweaty, mountain of a man tackles her, and they both go down face-first into gravel and broken glass. It tears at her skin, and she's grateful for the pain—it means she's alive. It means there's hope of escape. Of survival.

Where the fuck is Errol?

Yanked to her feet by a firm hand pulling at her underarm, she's dragged back to the line, and the tire is returned to her neck. She's still searching for another opportunity to run, to get the fuck outta there, even as the cadaverous teenager reappears from the shadows and touches a blazing torch to the tire. Fire blossoms, then darts like a living thing across Dorothea's gasoline-soaked clothes. Smoke fills her agonized lungs. She howls with her last breath as the flames dance over cracking and peeling skin. Within moments, her lips blister, tongue poking obscenely, the words lost, and she becomes engulfed. The air is white, then black.

Brain shutting down fast, the last thing Dorothea sees doesn't make sense: hundreds of insect-like legs emerging from the ground

MARC RUVOLO

to wriggle and dance in the orange flicker of firelight. The burning of her crisping skin, the searing of nerves and the blistering of her eyeballs meant she didn't know what she was seeing. Didn't care. Couldn't fathom what was happening, but the insects swarming around her somehow gave her peace.

The woman in the bike helmet flings her torch skyward, and it rises like a comet, only to plummet to earth moments later in a shower of dancing sparks.

"Let the feast begin!" she shrieks.

6

ONE

"THERE." HENRY CARRIED THE laptop to Digger and pointed at the screen. "The tag is pinging somewhere down by Marine Drive. That's my fucking car."

Legs tucked underneath him on the ratty leather couch, Digger took a pull off his vape, exhaling a cloud of fragrant white smoke. A glass bong and two more vapes lie close at hand on the scuffed-up black coffee table. "Okay. So, what are you gonna do about it?" He shrugged. "File a police report."

At some point the night before, Henry's beloved '98 Honda Civic had gone missing from the driveway. As a driver for food delivery apps, this was an unmitigated disaster. Without that car, he couldn't make money and couldn't afford rent or food. A month and he'd be homeless. He was already aware car theft in Portland was endemic, so he'd had a club on the steering wheel and an AirTag duct taped under the back bumper. The club hadn't deterred the thief, but the AirTag worked perfectly, showing him the car's location—a mostly-empty industrial area not far from the Columbia River.

He shook his head, sneering. "Fuck the fucking police. They're useless. You know that. I'm going to fucking get it back myself."

Digger offered up his usual goofy, stoned grin. "All right. I got your back then, tough guy." He laughed. "We can show these bitches a thing or two."

"Oh, I'm ready, bro. Let's look at a map."

Henry called up a Google map of Portland, zooming in on the area where the AirTag had pinged. It was north of where they were now, and aside from markers for a Frito Lay factory and a repo yard, the map was blank, a digital gray wilderness.

"Jesus, not a lot there," Digger said, getting up from the couch. "What is it, just...forests, you think?"

"Trees, yeah, but probably industrial wasteland. Homeless camps, maybe a dump, and who knows what else." Henry traced a finger across the screen. "This road that dead ends in the middle of nowhere is the closest you can drive. That's where we need to go. Guess we'll have to hike it from there."

"Wow, never thought there was so much...I dunno...like, *emptiness* out there. Shit like that creeps me out. Need a beer?" Digger was headed toward the kitchen.

Henry watched his friend go. "Yeah. Grab me one."

His anxieties were on full blast tonight. *If I died tomorrow, do you think he would give a shit? I doubt it.*

He and Digger had been friends since they were twelve. They'd lived in this house seven years now, always together, rarely apart. From the way they bickered, people thought they were an old married couple—but they weren't. Digger was straight, and as for Henry—well, Henry was an idiot who thought that if he just *tried a little harder*, just held in there *a bit longer*, then his straight friend would wake up to the fact that they were destined to be together. And that's what he'd done since high school. Wished, hoped, and prayed to the fucking patron saint of lost causes. Some days he could barely look at himself in the mirror.

How many times had he seriously considered suicide, only to chicken out? Yet another thing he'd failed at. Such a strange, detached conversation to have with oneself, a ghoulish monologue weighing facts, evidence, and emotion—an argument where a win was a loss, the thought process alternately engrossing and excruciating. Every day, he poked at the idea like you would a hangnail, satisfied by the low-grade pain it produced. At least feeling pain meant he was still alive.

Now thirty-two, his life had fallen into a meaningless rut, one deep enough that he couldn't see himself ever crawling out, but not deep enough to drown in. College had been a bust. His many bands had gone nowhere, and he had no partner, no savings, and no marketable skills. Chubby, balding, with all the charm of a sixteen-year-old, gummy-eyed shelter cat, even the old trolls on the hook-up apps passed him by without a second look. That left Henry with an ancient car and a stupid, unrequited crush on his only friend, who was so straight and oblivious and infuriating it was almost physically painful. Digger loved to pick up random cougars in the seedier bars on Hawthorne and bring them home, screwing the roof off into the early morning hours. Sheer, unadulterated torture for Henry, so most nights he self-medicated, drinking and smoking himself into oblivion.

Digger returned from the kitchen and handed over a sweating can. "Natural Lite. All we got left."

"Thanks, man."

The Civic being stolen should have pushed him closer to the end, but it was doing the exact opposite. The morose, tar-pit depression was fading, replaced by a giddy, white-hot anger, and the determination to live long enough to see justice done. He had nothing, and no one, but any fucker who would steal from someone so poor, so miserable, so—so *useless*, deserved every lousy, painful thing they had coming their way. Death? Sure, if it came down to that. And if Henry had anything to say about it, he would be the one to dole it out. He was that fed up—fed up enough to kill.

Life was overrated, and who gave a shit, anyway?

Digger grabbed his sandalwood stash box and reloaded the filthy bong. He worked as a healthcare assistant at an old folk's home, so he always had plenty of cash—content to spend every weekend drinking beer, getting high, and playing *World of Warcraft*. He took a deep lungful and then passed the bong to Henry.

"When can we go?" Henry asked, lighter poised over the bowl.

Digger blinked and smiled, his eyes slitted red. "Whenever you want, buddy. I just gotta get my gun out from my dad's safe. So say, tomorrow morning, like, after brunch?"

"That'll work." Henry fired up the bowl, clearing the chamber and holding the smoke for as long as he could before exhaling. The blood rushed to his head, and he exploded into a prolonged coughing fit, face beet red.

"Why do you always do that?" Digger snickered, snatching the bong from his hand. "You're a freakin' trip, man."

Two

Shocks creaking over rain-filled potholes, Janelle pulled the ancient Ford wagon into the asphalt lot of the Parkrose Pub. The fifth Portland bar she'd visited since arriving in town just a few days prior, the Parkrose was an ugly, dilapidated, brown shack, most likely built sometime in the late seventies. Killing the engine, she lit up a Marlboro Light and stared at the fogged glass door, a drive-thru order of Taco Bell still in the bag cooling on the passenger seat beside her. She'd been hungry when she bought it, but the thought of eating now made her queasy. Portland had a funny way of making you hungry and then killing your appetite.

It was early afternoon, and the bar was empty. Near the back, a baby-faced bartender sat staring up at a baseball game on one of the TVs, the sound muted, a plate of French fries and a pack of Camels on the bar top next to him.

She took one of the stools. "Can I get a Coke, please?" It was too early for beer. If she started now, the whole day would be wasted.

"Comin' up."

Janelle paid for the drink with her debit card. "Wanna leave it open?" the man asked. Both of his ears were pierced. Tiny diamond studs.

"No, thanks." Once he'd run the card, she signed and tipped him a dollar.

"Hey, wondering if you could help me." Janelle pulled a sheaf of folded papers from the back pocket of her jeans. "I'm looking for my sister. Last we spoke she said she was living here in northeast Portland. There's a picture. Maybe you've seen her?"

The bartender squinted at the creased computer printout. A silver cross peeked from the thatch of curly black hair spilling from his green tank top. "No, I can't say... Uh, wait, yeah, that's Dana, I think. Errol's girl."

"That's my sister, *Dorothea*. She's never gone by Dana. Did you say Errol, though? Errol Sanchez?"

"Dana's the name they told me." He shrugged. "And I don't know Errol's last name. A tall fella with tattoos, skinny as a stripper's pole, and twice as greasy." He chuckled at his joke. "They used to come in here and play the machines a little, but I haven't seen either of them for a while. Dana was a sweetheart, I hope nothing bad's happened to her."

Errol was tall and skinny and had tattoos. It was the best lead so far. "Do you know where they were staying?"

"They didn't have a place. Dana said they were livin' in a tent down by Laurelhurst Park. But the city and the cops been clearin' those camps every few weeks, regular now. Don't know if they'd still be there."

"Laurelhurst Park. Where's that, exactly? Close by? Sorry, I'm not from here."

"Southeast a couple miles, off Cesar Chavez. Take a right out of the parking lot, then left on Chavez, it's also called 39th. Laurelhurst is a big-ass, beautiful park, can't miss it, and you'll see the tents if they're there."

"Great. Thanks."

Back in the Escort, Janelle lit up another cigarette, watching the nonstop traffic zip past. Drizzle spattered the windshield, and she rolled up the window. It technically wasn't that cold, but she felt like she was freezing, the constant chilly dampness in the air about as far from Florida as you could get. Maybe that's why Dorothea came here. Janelle wasn't even sure what she'd say if she found her. Mama's dead? You can come home now? Did it even matter? All she wanted was to see her older sister, hug her, and confirm she was okay. Then, once they'd said everything they needed to say, well...maybe Portland had room for them both. Or maybe not. Maybe there was somewhere else for her out there, somewhere halfway between the two rotten coasts, somewhere she could sit

15

and smoke, find work, an apartment of her own, and get on with whatever came next.

Janelle stubbed out her cigarette in the ashtray and started the car.

THREE

By the time Henry cajoled a hungover Digger out of his bed, it was close to noon. "Brunch" had turned into "soggy breakfast sandwiches from the Jack drive-thru", *and* they still had to drive by Digger's father's house in Woodstock to get the gun.

"I feel like complete shit," Digger moaned, sitting slumped in the driver's seat of the Kia, cradling a thirty-ounce sweet tea between his thighs. The Sportage was practically brand-new, with a decal on the bumper that had always made Henry cringe a little: an assault rifle with the word OREGUNIAN. It was prime Digger.

"Come on, man." Henry knew this was going to happen and had prepared. "You promised me. Without a car, I'm fucked, dude. You know that. I can't pay rent. We got to get it back."

Digger grimaced, putting the car in drive. *"All right.* Fuck. Just, just...don't say anything until we get there, okay?"

Across town, they found Digger's father, Jack, standing in the weed-choked yard of his blue Craftsman trimming a half-dead hedge. A big man who loved cheap whiskey, his ropy muscles gone to fat, Jack had been on disability as long as Henry could remember. Luckily, he'd also inherited the house and a bit of cash from his grandparents. Enough to keep him in Jim Beam, frozen dinners, video poker, and lingerie bars, which was all he cared about anyway. Digger's mom had divorced Jack ages ago, moving back East to be with her sister. Digger called her on the holidays, but that was all, as she refused to set foot in Portland ever again. And considering all the lying and running around Jack had done while they were together, Henry didn't blame her one bit.

"Hey! Haven't seen you for a while." Jack grinned; teeth stained yellow and brown from a half-century of smoking roll-ups. The clippers he was using were bent and rusted, the wooden handles wrapped with frizzy duct tape. "What's up with that hair, Ben? All the pot you guys smoke finally turn you into Deadheads?"

Digger frowned. He *hated* his real name. "Haha. Good one, dad. I'm here to get one of my guns."

"Well, they're in the safe, like always. Combo's still the same. Which one you takin'?"

"The thirty-eight."

"What for? Elephant hunt? Drive-by?"

"Me and Henry wanna go shoot some targets at the range."

"Okay." He shrugged. "There's ammo in there too, take what you want but leave me at least two boxes, okay?"

"Sure thing. Thanks."

Three old, skinny mutts Jack kept locked up inside met them at the door, long claws clacking on the wooden floorboards, a furry mass of slapping tails, and insistent whining. "Damn it, get back!" Digger pushed the dogs off as they pressed against his legs.

The smallest one, a gray schnauzer, sniffed Henry's pant leg with intense interest, and he patted its wiry head. "Does he ever take them on walks?"

"Nah. Just lets them shit in the backyard. They seem happy enough, though. They get to sleep in his bed, and he overfeeds them. Better livin' here than over at the shelter, I guess."

Digger led him down a flight of stairs into the finished basement. Ducking around a pool table thick with dust, he pulled aside a beaded curtain revealing a steel door secured with three padlocks. Once he'd removed the last padlock, he shook his head. "Same combo for all of them. Big brain time."

Behind the door lay a deep closet, more like a walk-in pantry. Digger clicked the light switch. The closet was filled with dozens of weapons: guns, swords, knives, crossbows—lethal tools of every shape, size, and configuration.

"Always cold as shit down here," Digger muttered, stepping inside.

Henry gazed in awe at the vast arsenal. It was like a fabled treasure-house of weaponry, a dragon's horde of toxic masculinity. Jack was a 2A fanatic who had gifted Digger a gun every birthday since he was fourteen. "Dang. Which ones are yours?"

"The camo AR," he replied, pointing as he named them. "That 12-gauge with the brown stock, two of those Glocks, the Colt 1911, that .22 rifle 'bunny murderer', my first gun, the silver PPK, that cool old Nazi Luger, which I got when I turned twenty-one, the Weatherby Vanguard, and uh, ah, yes,"—he took a snub-nosed, matte black pistol from the shelf and brushed it clean—"my favorite, the thirty-eight special. Perfect for scaring off meth-head car thieves."

"Wow. Can I hold it?"

Digger made sure the cylinder was empty before handing Henry the pistol. "Don't point it at anyone. It's unloaded but has no safety. I'm gonna get some bullets."

Henry held the gun up to the light, admiring the finish. He'd never been, like so many other boys, obsessed with weapons and war, but holding the .38 and being here with Digger in this weird, hyper-male, inner sanctum stirred something inside of him. How romantic would it be to fight and die for your buddy... He sighted along the barrel and then squeezed the trigger—

"*Gimme that.*" Digger snatched the gun from his hand. "*Never* dry fire a pistol, you dumb moron."

"Sorry! I didn't know. Did I break it?"

"No, it's not broken." He polished the gun on his shirttail, then placed it in a small leather holster with Velcro straps. "Wait. You didn't know that?"

Henry shrugged. "I've never fired a gun in my life."

"No wonder you don't talk to your parents. That's like...child abuse." Digger knelt and strapped the holster around his ankle. "I'll teach you to shoot sometime if you want. Come on, let's go get this over with."

Digger hesitated at the bottom of the basement stairs. "Shit." He dug into his jacket pocket and pulled out a freezer bag filled with what looked like an ounce of bright green weed. "Here. Can you hold this for me? I took it out of the safe for us."

Henry took the bag. "What. Is Jack gonna frisk you before we leave?"

"You never know. Dude is unpredictable. Although, he's got so much bud he won't notice it's gone. And he'd never touch you."

Jack was sitting in a ratty La-Z-Boy on the junk-filled porch with the dogs lolling around his ankles, a sweating Bud Lite tallboy on the railing next to him. "You guys good?" he asked.

Digger clomped down the steps without stopping. "Locked it all back up," he said. "Thanks. See ya soon."

"I'm having my annual Fourth of July bar-b-que on Dan's dock in Scappoose, like usual," Jack called as they made for the fence. "Bring some pretty girls and I'll feed you and get you drunk."

"Will do, Dad," Digger said, climbing into the Kia.

Henry put on his seatbelt and then took out his Samsung Galaxy for directions. "Please don't make me go to that bar-b-que again. Worst brisket I ever ate. Like frickin' boot leather. Should be a crime treating an honest piece of meat like that."

Digger put the car into gear and hit the gas. "Shit. Tell me about it."

FOUR

THE HOUSELESS RESIDENTS OF Laurelhurst Park queued at the back of a maroon PT Cruiser receiving burritos and mini bottles of water from an elderly woman in denim overalls. Janelle parked her car in front of a huge, gated house—more of a beautiful mansion—where she could easily keep an eye out for her sister. A few stragglers arrived and the queue peaked then dwindled, with no sign of Dorothea, or Errol. Grabbing her woolen hat, she stepped out onto the sidewalk and locked the car. There was a break in the constant drizzle and the people hadn't dispersed, they were standing under the trees eating their burritos. It was now or never. She approached the person closest, a thin brown man wearing pink rubber boots, and unfolded her sister's picture.

"Hi," she said brightly, holding up the paper. "I'm looking for my sister, Dorothea. She also might be going by the name Dana, and her boyfriend, Errol. Tall guy with tattoos? Someone said they had a tent here. Have you seen them?"

"You see I'm eatin'?" The man gave her a hard look.

"Sorry." She backed away, moving on to the next person, a man who was bare-chested despite the wet chill, clad only in a worn leather vest sewn with biker patches. He smiled, but not with his eyes, blinking at the picture as she went through her whole spiel.

"Naw. I don't know her. But I'd like to know you. Wanna share my burrito?" He held it out, lettuce and rice falling to the ground. "It's good and all, but I hate the taste of cilantro, don't you?"

"No thanks," she said, stepping away. "I ate already."

He shrugged. "Your loss. I got good weed, and more, if you get my meaning."

The woman in denim overalls was packing up her car. When she saw Janelle coming, she shut and locked the rear hatch. "I'm all out of burritos honey, sorry. I have bottles of water, and there's some tortilla chips left."

"No thank you." She held up the paper. "I'm looking for my sister. She had a tent here. Have you seen her?"

The woman studied the picture. "I have. That's Dana. Goes around with Psychobilly Errol. But I heard she left town. Went home to Florida. I do know Errol got himself a used RV and last I saw it he'd parked it in the camp on 33rd and Marine."

Went home. To Florida? Now, wouldn't that be a kick in the teeth if Janelle had crossed the continent just for them to miss each other by a few days? "That's down by the river, right?"

"Yeah, the Columbia. The RVs all park on the side of the road there. Hasn't been cleared yet. It's by the National Guard Armory."

"Okay. Thank you. I'll check it out."

"If you can't find his RV, he also likes to hang out at a bar on the water. The Compass and Sextant. Good luck finding your sister."

Janelle returned to her car. Suddenly starving, she unwrapped one of the tacos from the bag on the passenger seat and wolfed it down. It was cold and congealed, disgusting, like she'd imagined it would be. The ice in the Coke had melted, but it still washed away most of the taste.

A Marlboro did the rest.

It was already getting dark. Janelle felt wrung out, with no energy left to search for Errol's RV today. It would have to wait until morning. The Motel Six Extended Stay was depressing, filled with old junkies and people just beginning their descent, but she'd bought a half pint of cheap vodka and a bottle of pineapple juice on the way back to smooth her time in the dingy room. With a stiff drink on the nightstand, she crawled beneath the bleached motel sheets and clicked the remote until she found the Home Shopping Network channel.

With the cable show droning in the background, Janelle practiced telling Dorothea she had their dead mama's ashes in a cardboard box in the trunk of her car. Would she cry? Laugh? Walk away? It was one of the reasons she was here. The cremains tied Janelle to the past, like a yoke around her neck—one she hoped her older sister might help her finally remove. Dorothea had run from their mother's abuse, but now their mother was dead. No power there anymore. Together, the sisters could finally exorcise Regina from their lives. She choked down the plastic cup of sticky sweet vodka and pulled the covers up to her neck. Her eyelids drooped.

"...it's the go anywhere, clean anything, cordless vacuum. And it can be yours for only five payments of fifty-nine, ninety-five. You heard that right, an incredible deal for an appliance of this caliber, just five payments of fifty-nine, ninety-five..."

FIVE

"YOU THINK WE COULD stop and get a six-pack?" Digger asked. They were on Marine Drive past the airport, stuck between two semis, and traveling east toward Gresham. Henry rolled down the window, taking a deep lungful of the relatively fresher river air.

"There are only restaurants down here. We could stop for a quick beer and a shot. I know Salty Sam's is up ahead."

Digger shook his head. "Too posh. I don't want a fifteen-dollar Manhattan. How about the Compass and Sextant? That bar next to the beach?"

"Okay." Henry stared out over the expanse of dark green river. It was busy, the choppy water crowded with windsurfers, jet skis, and small pleasure craft. "I've never been there."

A few miles down the road, Digger pulled the Kia into the gravel parking lot of a squat, weathered building with a sloping roof. The patio was filled with drinkers hunkering under beach umbrellas.

Frayed pennants flapped in the brisk river breeze. They parked and got out, the strong scent of fried food and tidal mud in the air.

Walking up to the door, Henry got a clearer look at the people drinking on the patio: boomers, bikers, and any number of other haggard, unfriendly types. "You sure about this?" he asked.

Digger made a face. "It's only one drink. *And*...maybe some cheese sticks."

Inside was dimly lit, with a vaguely generic nautical theme, lots of coiled rope, and taxidermy fish. The ghost of decades-old cigarette smoke lingered in the fittings and grimy woodwork. Digger approached the bar.

"Hi, can I get two Bud Lights and two shots of whatever the well whiskey is."

The lank-haired bartender frowned, looking up from her phone to squint at his license. "Sure thing. I'm gonna need to see your friend's ID, too."

Drinks in hand, they found a table at the back and Henry sat to check his phone. "The AirTag's moved again. Not far, maybe a half mile east. But deeper into no-man's-land. Shit. This is gonna suck. What are they doing? Off-roading with my car?"

"It might be stripped already." Digger downed his shot and grimaced, chasing it with a swig of beer. "Who knows what condition it's in."

"Please don't fucking say that. I need to stay positive, okay?"

"Okay. Staying positive. We'll find it." He got up from the table. "I'm gonna play some video poker."

The beer and shot went straight to Henry's head and bladder. "Takin' a piss," he said to Digger as he passed him on the way to the bathroom.

Digger held up his empty bottle. "Another round?"

"No! We have to leave. You said just one."

The men's facilities consisted of a glazed urinal trough, almost rusted through at the bottom, and a line of antique sinks. The acrid scent of beer piss was strong. How many thousands of gallons had passed through these grotty drains over the decades? A man stood at the end of the urinal, so Henry took his place as far away as possible and unzipped. With a grunt of satisfaction, the man finished up and sauntered to the sink, whistling under his breath as he ran the water. A cloud of steam rose to fog the scratched-up mirror.

The man was quite tall, late forties, arms inked with jailhouse tattoos, his greasy black pompadour shot through with threads of gray. Out of the corner of his eye, Henry saw him turn away from the sink and dry his hands on the hem of the moth-eaten Black Sabbath tour T-shirt he was wearing.

"More than three shakes is considered playing with it, you know."

Henry zipped up quickly. "What's that?"

"Nothin'." The man chuckled. "Just a dumb joke." He offered his hand. "I'm Eddie, what's your name?"

The hand was huge, knuckles gnarled, calloused, and still slightly damp. Pink from the hot water. He gave it a brief squeeze and pulled away. "Henry."

"I never seen you around here before."

"No. It's my first time."

"Welcome. Been comin' to the old Compass for twenty years now. Good place. Everyone's welcome here." Eddie made a smacking sound with his meaty lips. "You wanna smoke some weed?"

Surprised by the stranger's offer, Henry nearly did a double take. "I... Uh, naw. I'm good, thank you. I got someone waitin' on me, it was nice to meet you, Eddie."

"Oh, *boyfriend*?"

Now this was getting uncomfortable. "No. Just a friend. My car got stolen and we're going to look for it."

"Mmm hmm, lots of that going around. Crooks and cheats everywhere these days, I'm afraid. That's why people like you and me need to look out for each other."

Henry took a halting step back. "People like...you and me?"

"Gays. Handsome boy like you deserves a good daddy. To protect him, buy him things."

"Seriously, I'm fine." He eyed the door. "Friend probably thinks I fell in. You have a good day."

"Oh, I will. You, too. And if you're ever looking to hang out, I'm always around here. Don't be a stranger."

Henry was already halfway out of the bathroom. "I won't. Thanks!"

Digger was back at the table pulling apart a matchbook, looking bored. Henry breezed right by him, waving frantically. "Oh jeez, come on, let's go, we gotta go. Now."

SIX

JANELLE WOKE TO ANGRY shouts from outside. Creeping from the warmth of the motel bed, she peeked through the curtain. Two men were fighting in the parking lot. They grappled on the asphalt in the early morning sunshine, clothes wet and muddy. One had lost a sneaker. A sallow-faced woman sat huddled with two small children inside a late-model station wagon, watching the men fight. One of the children, a girl still in her princess PJs, burst into tears, wailing for her daddy. The other child soon followed suit.

Back in bed, Janelle eyed the remaining vodka and pineapple juice. The men were still shouting and cursing. A siren sounded in the distance. Pancakes, that's what she needed right now. A big, fluffy stack slathered in butter. Not more vodka. *Pancakes*. With a groan, she got up and padded into the cold bathroom to take a shower.

An hour later, she was parked next to a McDonald's, a Styrofoam container in her lap. The pancakes were gritty and lukewarm, a disappointment, but the black coffee was blistering hot, and once she'd downed the whole cup and smoked a cigarette, she finally felt ready to face the world.

The mapping app on her phone indicated that 33rd and Marine Drive was about four miles away, on the river, and aside from the airport, there didn't seem to be much else there. She didn't relish seeing Errol again, they'd never been friends, but it seemed like the only way to find out the truth of where Dorothea had gone.

Dana. Why would her sister be using a fake name? What had she gotten into? She and Errol had partied back in Fort Lauderdale, but it had been mostly vanilla stuff—booze, pot. Well...and meth sometimes. Had they moved on to harder stuff? They were living on the streets after all.

Wan sunlight peeked through the clouds as she drove, brightening things up a bit. The app had routed her through an industrial corridor, a mini highway lined with factory complexes, auto junkyards, trucking hubs, and a few forlorn trailer parks, which only added to the feeling of complete desolation. Tent camps sprouted on the empty lots like mushrooms after a spring rain, colorful debris washed up on the banks of a raging, capitalist river. A man darted out into the street while she waited at a stoplight, waving a two-by-four, but the light changed in time, and she managed to speed away unharmed. After that, she made sure all the doors were locked.

The size of the RV camp on 33rd came as a shock. She'd expected maybe a handful of vehicles, but many dozens were parked along the side of the road for almost a mile in either direction. Some were well-kept, others not so much, their windows boarded up, surrounded by heaps of trash and discarded furniture. A few were burned out entirely, charred hulks decorated with incomprehensible graffiti. Janelle pulled over, uncertain how she'd even go about finding which trailer was Errol's. Would she need to walk around, knocking on every strange door?

A white pick-up truck passed, driving slowly, not police, but with strobing lights on the roof and black, block lettering on the doors: CITY OF PORTLAND. THE CITY THAT WORKS. Janelle followed it. A half mile up, the truck pulled over next to an RV sitting alongside a particularly large pile of abandoned trash. Two men got out of the truck, and each took an end of a sodden, piss-stained mattress from the pile, tossing it into the bed. She waved cheerily as she walked up to them.

"Excuse me!"

The city workers stopped what they were doing to stare at her, their faces blank.

"Hi, sorry to bother you. I'm looking for a man that parks here—"

35

"We don't talk to nobody that lives here," the older man cut her off. "Can't help you."

A woman hung her head out the window of the RV. "You assholes in my stuff again?" Her face was bloated; pale pink lipstick and raccoon eyes under a mop of greasy brown curls. "I *told* you to fucking stop it."

The men ignored her, continuing to carry trash from the pile and load it into the truck bed.

She dangled a half-smoked cigarette out the window, squinting at Janelle. "I heard you askin' these overpaid jag-offs about a man. Who ya lookin' for honey? Your daddy? A boyfriend?" The woman ashed on the ground. "I know most everybody around here."

"I'm looking for my sister, Dorothea. She might be going by the name Dana and she's with a man called Errol Sanchez. Someone told me he parks his RV down here."

She shook her head. "What's he look like?"

"Uh, real tall and skinny, older, he's got a lot of tattoos, and kind of an old-timey, Elvis hairdo."

"Hmm. Sounds like Eddie. He just started parkin' here a few weeks ago. His Winnebago is up closer to the water by the National Guard thingy. On this same side here. It's all spray-painted up, so you can't miss it. He's got a car, too. A blue Monte Carlo."

That was Dorothea's car. She'd bought it with money saved up working at the Dollar General by their house in Tampa. It had to be them. "Thank you so much, I appreciate it."

"No sweat, cutie. Good luck."

Someone had spray-painted "asshole" and "groomer" in big, red letters on the side of the seventies-era Winnebago. Then someone else had crossed them out and written in even bigger letters: CANDY WAGON. Janelle parked across the street and lit up. She stayed in her car, dreading having to knock on the RV's door. The Monte Carlo was not there. After she'd been watching for ten minutes, a man wearing golf shoes, and a white cowboy hat wandered over and tapped on her window.

"Whatcha lookin' for?" he asked, darting twitchy glances over his shoulder. "I got everything."

She cracked the window an inch. "No thanks. I'm here to see Eddie. I don't think he's home, though."

The man pushed back his sweat-stained hat, revealing a puckered white scar on his forehead. "Door on the Candy Wagon is always open. You can go in and wait. He'll be back soon."

"Do you know if Dana is around? Or Dorothea?"

"Never heard of 'em." Somewhere nearby a dog began to bark, the high and piercing yaps of something small, like a Chihuahua or Jack Russell. "Shit." His head went up. "Gotta go."

Janelle watched in her rearview mirror as the man clomped down the road before disappearing into a stand of stunted pine trees. Once he was gone, she got out, locked her car, and walked around to the door of the spray-painted Winnebago. She knocked, waited, and when no one answered, grabbed the door latch. It was unlocked, just like the man in the cowboy hat had said.

Expecting to find a mess, a drug den maybe, Janelle was surprised at how clean and tidy it was inside. There was a couch with floral pillows and a folded Afghan, a new flatscreen TV, and some thriving houseplants. The bed was made, and the matching duvet and pillowcases were freshly laundered. Still, it didn't look like anyone *lived* there. It looked like a motel room or a movie set. A familiar-looking Bible lay on the counter behind the driver's seat, and Janelle picked it up. Inside the cover, someone had inscribed their name in florid longhand: R. Molina.

Regina Molina.

This was one of their *mother's* Bibles.

It wasn't surprising Dorothea had taken the Bible when she ran away. Even though religion brought them nothing but misery and heartache, she had doggedly held on to her faith. Not their mother's twisted version of faith, one made up of equal parts guilt, fear, and pain, but faith in the true teachings of Jesus—compassion, and forgiveness. Love. Faith had helped her survive the abuse, and she'd used the Bible as a shield. Regina may have failed to crush the independent spirit of either daughter, but it was not for lack of trying. Janelle could never forgive her for the hell she put them through, but maybe now that Regina was gone, she could learn to forget it ever happened, to wipe clean those hard years.

Each evening before bed, Regina, *the Queen*, ordered her daughters to kneel on a hardwood plank, hands clasped, and listen while she read scriptures. She chose verses that warned of damnation and hellfire, all the terrible things that awaited little girls who didn't mind their mothers. Sometimes Dorothea would giggle in the middle of the reading, which would in turn make Janelle giggle, and then they both would be whipped with a switch. If they showed any defiance after that, they were beaten again, and then locked inside a spider-infested shed out in the garden.

Janelle replaced the Bible. If it *was* Regina's, and it looked to be, that meant Dorothea had been here, too. It also meant Eddie and Errol were the same person. Had her sister lived here with him at some point? It didn't look like it, there were no clothes, or food, no personal effects at all.

"Well, *hello* there, Janny-girl. What a surprise to find you here in my humble abode."

That voice sent prickles down her spine. She hadn't heard the car pull up. "Hey...Errol. Or is it Eddie, now? Running from something, again?"

Errol laughed, placing a six-pack of beer on the counter. "Still spittin' venom. You Molina girls sure do like to be on top, so y'all can do the ridin'. It's okay though, I'm a sucker for it."

"Yeah, sure." Errol looked repulsive as ever with his too-long arms and legs, and drooping, hound dog face. A beat-up, Stretch-Armstrong Elvis Impersonator. "I'm looking for Dorothea. Her cell is disconnected. Where is she?"

He pulled up his grubby T-shirt to scratch his pale belly. "Welp. Dorothea went back home. Said she didn't like it here. Too cold, too much rain. I begged her to stay, but you know how she is."

"To Tampa? When?"

"No. Said she was gonna kip with a gal pal in Clearwater. Few weeks ago, now. We was livin' in a welfare hotel, then she dumped me, so I moved in here. Friend sold me this RV on the cheap after that." He glanced at the sweating six-pack. "Hey, you fancy a beer?"

"No, thank you. So, I asked around and people mentioned she was using the name Dana. And now you're Eddie. What's that all about?"

"My, you are the cutest little detective, aren't you?" He pulled a can from the six-pack and popped the tab. "What's it about? Not much. We needed new names to get us food stamps. I had a job lined up, but it fell through. Dorothea was feeling poorly, her stomach troubles, you know, and couldn't work. Around here, welfare is easier to get if you ain't had it before."

Like always, he had a vaguely plausible answer for everything. This was a dead end. Her sister wasn't here, and there was no way to prove she *hadn't* gone home like he said. "Do you have her new number? Some way she left to get in touch?"

"Nope. Like I said, she broke up with me. Dumped. Abandoned. I have the same number you have. Y'know, I never understood why you and I couldn't at least be friends, Janny. Am I that bad of a guy?"

"Come on Errol, you know the litany of shit you've pulled. Has any of that changed?"

He took a long pull off the can. "Well, no. But your sister saw something in me, didn't she? I can't be all that terrible. I'm a loyal friend." He did a drunken twirl, bumping into the driver's chair. "And a good dancer, too. Why not have just one, little, beer with me for old time's sake, darlin'?"

"I said, no. And if you can't help me find my sister, I'll be going."

He lifted an eyebrow. "Back to Florida, to Regina, and that house o' horrors? Shocked she let you come here."

"Well, for your information, our mother passed. It's what I came to tell Dorothea."

"Oh, what a *shame*," he said, voice dripping with sarcasm. He crunched the empty can, throwing it on the floor. "I hear Hell is especially hot and muggy this time of year."

"You're an asshole."

"Aw, don't be that way. Let me buy you some fish and chips. A nice dinner, and then we part ways. An apology for the past."

Feeling uneasy with how insistent he was being, Janelle stepped toward the open door. "No. I've got to go."

Errol moved quickly, engulfing her in his ropy orangutan arms before she could even cry out. He flipped around behind, putting her in a chokehold, a terrible pressure on her neck. She could smell the cloying sweetness of his strange odor. Clawing at his iron grip, Janelle struggled to breathe as darkness crowded the corners of her vision.

"I tol' yah we could be friends, Janny-girl," Errol grunted, tightening his hold. "Now it's time to get up close and personal."

SEVEN

THE KIA FLEW EASTWARD down Marine Drive, following the turns of the broad, shimmering river. Tents and tumbledown shacks lined the stony bank of the Columbia, makeshift camps strewn with garbage and stripped cars. A faded American flag hung from a tilted pole, ragged ends snapping in the brisk breeze.

"He said you were handsome?" Digger laughed. "Was this man by any chance carrying a white cane?"

Henry folded his arms over his chest. "Fuck you, dude. It seriously creeped me out."

"Maybe you should have given him a chance. You know, being a single *gay* and all."

"Oh, shut up." Henry looked at his phone. "Shit! The AirTag! The signal is gone!"

"Relax." Digger seemed nonplussed. "We know where it was. We can still go there and look around."

43

"Do you think they found it? The AirTag?"

"Who?"

"The thieves, you dumb ass! They probably destroyed it so we can't track the car!"

"Or there's just limited service. Doesn't that thing need a signal to work?"

Henry stared at his phone. "Ah, I didn't think of that. It works on Bluetooth, but how do you get Bluetooth in the ass-middle of nowhere?"

"Exactly. So just relax. We'll be out there in ten minutes, tops."

Digger left Marine Drive, turning the Kia into an empty street lined with faceless warehouses. Trucks idled in the docking bays, mini factories belching pale smoke into the sky. Sad saplings sagged between the sidewalks, holding on for dear life to the sticks and twine that kept them erect in such inhospitable terrain. How anything grew here was a mystery, what little of nature remained appeared poisoned, salted, unfit for anything other than toxic waste and unfettered commerce.

The street dead-ended at a huge asphalt parking lot fenced with razor wire. A rusted boat trailer with two flat tires lay abandoned near the gate. Digger rolled to a stop on the gravel shoulder, and they both got out.

"I think it was that way." Henry pointed at the trees. A small forest, but one filled with muddy trails and ribbons of strewn garbage. Digger nodded, vape in hand. "After you."

They had to cross a deep drainage ditch to access the tree line. Bleached animal bones littered the wet, weedy mudhole, and they picked their way over the driest spots, trying to protect their shoes from the worst of the foul-smelling muck. The air here tasted especially thick and polluted, and Henry's throat became sore.

Several hand-drawn signs hung from the trees on the far side of the ditch. A.C.A.B., STAY OUT FUCKFACE, PIG HUNTING ZONE, SMOKE UP AND LIVE, PRAISE THE FEAST!!! And strangest of all: KOLCHAKS ONLY.

Henry touched the crudely painted cardboard. "What's a Kolchak?"

Digger pulled out his phone. "Let's see. Uh, nope. No service. Do you have service?"

Henry looked. "Yeah, one bar." He typed the word onto his phone. "*Kolchak: The Night Stalker*, it's a TV show from the seventies. Like a... *proto-X-Files*, I guess. Tweakers must have put it up as a dumb joke."

Under the trees, the first thing Henry noticed was how many used hypodermic needles littered the ground. Hundreds of discarded sharps, and possibly thousands of the little orange caps that accompanied them lay nestled in the gnarled roots, mixed with the pinecones, sticks, and leaf litter. He'd always been frightened of needles and only smoked heroin once before discovering it just wasn't for him. He liked cocaine a lot more and would gladly snort a line if offered (and it was free), but thankfully neither had become a habit. This here was something else though, clear evidence of full-blown, thermonuclear bacchanal, illicit drug use on an almost industrial scale.

Digger kicked a crushed beer can. "Jesus. Fuck this place. Glad I wore pants. Can you still pull up your maps?"

Henry looked at his phone and shook his head. "It's not loading. This is a mess. Who knows what craziness is out here? We won't go too far. Judging from that parking lot over there, this is around where the last Tag signal was. Keep an eye out for stray crackheads."

Two deep ruts in the forest floor wound through anemic stands of Douglas fir and hemlock indicating where cars had passed before. Every few yards they encountered heaps of random trash, bits and pieces of people's lives: phone chargers, paperback books, shoes, clothing, hydro flasks—and dozens of owner's manuals for Toyotas, Subarus, Hondas, Chevys, Teslas—stacks of soggy insurance and registration papers, all waterlogged, filthy, and trampled into the dirt. These items all told the same sad story: things a meth-head thief might discard from a recently stolen car.

Henry snatched up a bike helmet and flung it into the branches of a wilted dogwood tree. "How do they get away with this shit? Fucking druggy parasites."

"Cops don't give a shit." Digger fiddled with his elaborate vape. "You think they'd drag their lazy asses way the fuck out here?"

Henry stopped. "Wait. Hold up."

A yellow, flop-eared mutt appeared on the path ahead. No collar, no tags. Big paws caked with dried mud. The dog observed them dispassionately, his tail still. Henry extended a hand to the stray. "Hey, buddy, hey, doggy, we're friends, buddy. Hi, how you doin' pup?" He glanced at Digger, who retreated behind a tree. "You got any dog treats?"

"Why the fuck would I have dog treats?"

"Well, your dad has dogs. I don't know. You might."

"I don't."

Three more dogs padded out onto the path behind the lab. One of them, a red Pit bull, began growling, a low, menacing thrum deep inside his broad chest. A German Shepherd bared its teeth and snarled. The Shepherd was in bad condition, with one ear missing and its eyes leaking clear fluid. The Pit bull charged. Henry snatched up a dry, brittle pine branch as the dogs surged forward, and began swinging it at them. The dogs milled around, out of reach of the branch, tails tucked between their legs, ears pinned back.

"Fire a warning shot," Henry ordered, hefting the stick. "To scare them off."

"I'm not going to shoot if I don't have to. I've only got six bullets."

"What happened to the box of extra bullets we got?"

"I forgot it in the car." Digger shrugged. "I'm an idiot, okay?"

Henry swung the branch. "Shoo! Get out of here!"

The Pit bull snarled, and ignoring Henry's branch, ran for Digger.

"Shit!" Digger hopped on one foot, trying to get to his pistol.

Henry brought the stick down hard on the dog's back, and the dry wood broke into multiple fragments. The yellow mutt rushed him, jumping and snapping. Henry aimed a kick at its chest. "Get the fuck away, dog, go. Go!"

Too late, Digger gave up on the holster and tried to run, but the Pit was already on him, chomping down on his leg. Luckily, it only latched onto the hem of his bootcut jeans. With the sound of tearing fabric, the dog shook its blocky head back and forth. Digger tried to run in the opposite direction, but the Pittie locked his paws, stubbornly hanging on. Out of nowhere a frazzle-haired terrier started biting Digger's shoes.

He made another grab for the ankle holster, but the terrier snapped at his hand. "Fuck! Help me! Henry!"

Despite the show of fangs, the yellow mutt seemed more bark than bite. Henry kicked it again, this time connecting with its muzzle. The dog yelped piteously and turned tail into the bushes. But before he could go to Digger's aid, the earless German Shepherd rushed him, ready to join the fight.

A high-pitched, breathy, whistling filled the air and the shepherd's ear went flat. It looked around, letting out a low whimper, then bolted into the underbrush.

"What the hell?" Henry put his hands over his ears, trying to shut out the painful noise. It pulsed like a smoke alarm, sharp and piercing, making his jaw ache.

The Pit bull released Digger's cuff. Its eyes rolled, showing white, and then it too fled, whimpering into the azalea bushes. The remaining dogs followed close behind, a yelping, frightened pack.

The noise tapered off to a low-pitched buzz. Henry's heart hammered in his chest—it had all happened so damn fast—he'd never been attacked by dogs. Thank God they didn't get stoned. "What is that noise?"

Digger fingered the torn pant leg. If not for the ankle holster, the Pit bull's fangs might have easily found the pale, tender skin of his ankle. "This is insane, dude, those fucking mutts, I almost got bit! What if they had rabies or something? Let's get out of here. *Now.*"

"We'll only go a little further, I swear." Henry dropped the last bit of broken branch. "I need that car, man, or I'm dead. You know that. Please. Buddy. Digger. She's all I got in the world."

Digger regained his feet, dusting leaf litter from his clothes. "All right. But this is fucking stupid. Any more dogs like that, you're on your own."

The forest ruts ended at a weedy, trash-strewn slope. Below, a valley filled with the hulks of stripped cars, hundreds of them, a vast auto necropolis, stretched as far as the eye could see. A murder of crows circled overhead, cawing angrily as they dive-bombed something, or someone, hidden in the sprawling maze of wrecks.

Those closest to the slope remained relatively intact, but the deeper you went the more stripped and rusted the cars became. Henry was stunned. Someone was running a massive chop-shop operation. Sure, it was out in the middle of nowhere, but how was it possible to get away with something so blatantly criminal, for so long? Did Portland cops make any effort at all?

Digger exhaled a cloud of vape smoke. "What the hell."

Seeing movement, Henry grabbed his shoulder. "Shit. Get down. There's people over there."

Three women and a man were standing together on the far side of the valley, next to a faded yellow school bus. Two of the women carried what looked like long wooden flag poles, or maybe spears. The woman without a pole slapped at the man, who appeared visibly angry and upset.

"I don't like this, at all," Digger whispered. "Let's get the fuck out of here."

Henry was about to agree when someone cleared their throat behind them. "Well, well, what the fuck have I found here? Two frightened rabbits hiding in the grass. It *is* my lucky day."

Eight

...

... ...

... ... Uhhhh.

Thatwe'rerunningLordovertheskydowntoendsofthehunger-graspgraspingtheendsofthehungerhungerhunger...

Dorothea feels nothing, sleeps without dreaming, and then—!!!—an explosion of senses. And she feels...

Everything.

The slow curling roots of each tree and bush, chill rain as it spatters, trickling into the earth, every insect that crawls on the ground, every wriggling worm, every paw that pads softly in the loam, and all their hearts beating together like the drum of distant surf. Everything. *Everything*—all at once. Yet there are no eyes, no arms, no legs, no actual body. Is she dead? Undead? A charred corpse lying in a shallow grave? A confused ghost? No, no, no, no, she's awake.

Aware.

And there are images, and impressions, disembodied but real. Tactile. What is it she "sees", exactly?

...A network extending from the center of her consciousness, a million limbs that snake through the rebirthed world, neither up nor down, linked through connective tendrils, wild, feral, inexplicable. And she can travel within this network, a thought, an impulse, riding the golden pathways, a sparking spirit inside a wire. Dorothea follows the network, giddy, until she senses a breech in connection, dark spaces inhabited by something—other. Multiple *others*.

LordovertheskydowntoendsofthehungerafraidtoseewheretheendsuponendstotheLordtohungertohunger...

Beyond the babbling of these others, the network continues onward, outward, different pathways she can freely choose. She pauses here, befuddled by it all. Then the voices come, a crashing wall of words and syllables, a cascade of jarring, jumbled information, not heard *per se*, but *sensed*. No mouths, nor tongues, neither plosive nor fricative, but there is talking to it, syllables, timbre, and tone, information being exchanged in its rawest most instinctual form. With what, though, or who, she hasn't the slightest idea. It's overwhelming, a glut of sensory images, a streaming fountain of words, words, words...

WASTE GROUND

Thatwe'rerunningovertheskydowntoendsoftheLordhungergrasp-graspingtheendsofthehungerhungerhunger...

NINE

CHOKED OUT BY ERROL, Janelle fell unconscious long enough for him to get one of the steel cuffs around her wrist. When she came to and realized what he was doing, she kicked and flailed, but he jammed a sharp knee into the small of her back and wrenched her arm sideways until she quit struggling. Then he quickly clicked the other cuff around her wrist and threw her to the floor. Cursing him and his entire family, she pushed herself into a sitting position against the painted cabinets.

"You crazy fuck, get these off me! Help! Somebody help me!"

Errol hurried to the back of the Winnebago, returning with a pair of tube socks. "Oh, quit it, Janny-girl. These will have to do for your ankles. Don't you kick me now, ya hear?"

She did kick, but it was no use, and before long he had her ankles secured, too. Groping in her jean's pockets, he found her cell phone and took it.

"Help! Someone fucking help me!" she screamed again, trying to roll onto her side.

"Nobody's comin'." He leered; a huge, ugly smile plastered on his jowly face. "Lotta screams around here. Like birdsong, people just ignore it."

"What are you going to do to me, asshole?" She strained against the cuffs. "What do you want?"

"Oh, don't worry, I'm not touchin' you. Won't do nothin' to you, neither. Can't spoil the meat before the feast, as the Kolchaks say. You're worth way more to me whole. You're my next delivery, few more like you and Dorothea and I'll be travelin' back south in style. Trade up this beast here for a brand-new Class B."

"You're fucking batshit, Errol. What did you do to Dorothea? Let me go!"

Errol was at the Winnebago door. "Just calm down, Janelle. Jeez, you and your blessed sister. Yap, yap, yap. Never did learn when to shut up."

Janelle heard the engine turn over and the crunch of gravel as the RV began to move. Wriggling closer to the door, she got onto her knees but couldn't find a way to stand up. Instead, she forced her butt up onto the bench seat where she could see through a crack in the boards covering the windows. A sign at the side of the road whipped past: OREGON ARMY NATIONAL GUARD. They were heading toward the river. Janelle wrenched her legs, working them back and forth, trying to loosen the tube socks.

Less than ten minutes later the RV turned and rolled to a stop. She saw other parked cars through the window crack, and in the distance, the green, rippling waves of the Columbia. Errol got out and spoke with someone, a conversation she couldn't make out. Then the RV door opened, and he climbed back in.

"How'd you get up there?" He waggled a finger. "You don't give no more trouble now, hear?"

Another person entered. A middle-aged woman wearing fatigues, combat boots, and a black beret. Frizzy ginger dreads hung down her back, almost to the cracked leather belt girding her ample waist. She rubbed meaty brown palms together. "Anyone gonna miss her?"

Errol shook his head. "Nah. Another Florida gal. No daddy to speak of. Mama just died and flew off to Heaven."

"Another Florida gal? Just like the one you brought in last wee—"

Errol shook his head, making a shushing motion. "Let's get on with it, time is money, ya know."

Janelle heard music coming from somewhere outside of the RV. "Help! Somebody help me! Call the police! Help!"

Errol straddled her, placing his huge, smelly hand over her mouth and nose. "Hush, you."

The woman removed her beret and placed it on the counter, sucking brown teeth. "Where'd you snatch this one?"

"She came to me, if you can believe it. Was waitin' here in the Candy Wagon when I got home from errands. Just had to knock her down and cuff her up for ya. Boom, bap, here we are."

"Well, good. There's another feast in two days. The Cavity speaks through the penitents at least once a day now. We have people watching it 24/7 and writing it all down. Sarathi thinks if we offer food often enough it'll talk more. Answer questions. Tell us things."

Janelle struggled in Errol's grip, but he clamped down harder. She grew light-headed. Suffocating. "What sorts of things?" he asked.

The woman's watery blue eyes glistened. "Godhead things. Demon things. Immortality. Hell, maybe even the goddamn end of the fucking world."

TEN

DIGGER YELPED AND TOOK off running.

Henry tried to run after him but got tangled in his legs and sprawled face-first into the tall grass. Someone laughed. It sounded like a woman.

"What in God's green earth?" It was the voice that had spoken earlier.

"Weed smoking," the woman replied. "Makes your brain smooth as sea glass."

Henry rolled onto his back. The woman was older, mid-fifties, with salt-and-pepper braids and blue jean coveralls. She carried a spear, a ten-foot wooden pole with a forked end, a stark contrast to the man who stood beside her, who was a little person.

The little person smiled and offered his hand, and Henry was horrified to see the man's teeth had been filed into sharp yellow points. He tried not to recoil. "Took a tumble there, buddy. Relax," the man said. "We're not going to hurt you."

"Yeah," the woman with the pole laughed. "Bruce here doesn't bite."

Henry took his hand and got back on his feet. "Thanks," he said sheepishly. He looked around. "Where did my friend go?"

Bruce pointed at the trees. He was wearing brand new Nike Max Air sneakers and a child-sized Portland Thorns T-shirt. "He ran that way."

Henry shook his head. Stupid, stoned Digger. He better not have ditched out. "Shit."

"What are you guys doing way out here?" Bruce asked. "Didn't you see the signs by the road?"

Henry decided to be honest. "My, uh, my car was stolen, and I traced it to this area. I'm *poor*, dude. I need it to work. I've got to get it back. I'll be homeless in a month if I can't get that car."

Bruce made a sympathetic face. "Aw, that sucks. What kinda car?"

"A midnight blue '98 Honda Civic. Have you seen it?"

"Maybe." Bruce scratched the black bristles on his chin. "Rhoda, didn't we check out a new midnight blue Civic down by Uchoa's pile-up? Came in the last day or so?"

Rhoda took a cigarette butt from behind her ear. "Oh, yeah. I think we did. Would you like us to show you, kid?"

Henry waved at the trees, hoping Digger would see and understand that he wasn't in any danger from these people. "Yeah, that would be awesome. Thank you."

"You got cash? Uchoa won't let shit go without some kinda payment."

"No." His hand crept to his jacket pocket and the ounce Digger had given him to hold. "But I got weed I can trade."

Rhoda nodded. "Cool. Let's go, then."

Henry hesitated, wishing Digger would reappear. "What's that pole for?"

"Dealing with the dog packs." Rhoda waggled the thin staff for effect. "Scares 'em off. Also keeps 'em at bay if they run up on us."

"The Pile Up isn't far," Bruce said. "But we gotta go right now. We have a meeting soon."

"A meeting?" Henry almost laughed, imagining these two in a corporate boardroom. He glanced at the trees again. Nothing. Was Digger watching? "Okay. Take me there."

The unlikely pair led him down the grassy hill into the auto graveyard. They were strange, but *seemed* harmless enough, hippies, or crust punks—travelers, probably something along those lines. Besides, he could always outrun them, the old woman too fat to catch him, Bruce's legs too stubby. If things got dicey, he would haul ass back to Digger's car and try again later. Maybe it was stupid, suicidal even, but this time Henry was not going to be beaten.

The sheer quantity of gutted vehicles blew his mind, with many of them being brand new, not clunkers, but recent models. Expensive. None of this was being hidden. Probably could see it plain as day in the planes and helicopters that flew from the airport. It was like another world out here.

The Pile Up was just that, crushed cars piled on top of each other, some stacked four high. A line of stolen shopping carts, with mini oil slicks underneath each one, held the stripped parts. Henry looked around for a forklift or any heavy equipment. There was none. How had they managed it?

"Uchoa!" Bruce called out. "Where you at?"

A woman wearing grease-stained gray coveralls crawled out from under a smashed-up BMW. Henry found her strikingly attractive, Pacific Islander or Hawaiian maybe, with wide, full lips and a tumble of loose, jet-black hair. "What's up?" she asked, awkwardly reaching across her torso to push a filthy-looking rag into her pocket. It was only then Henry realized she was missing her left hand.

"This guy here has come looking for his car. Stolen, I guess. What did you say it was?"

"Midnight blue '98 Honda Civic." The ground suddenly trembled beneath his feet. Just a few seconds and then it was gone. "What was that?"

Bruce frowned. "What was what?"

"Felt like an earthquake."

"Hmm. I didn't feel anything. Did you?" Rhoda shrugged, shaking her head no.

Uchoa motioned with her stump for Henry to follow. "Come on, bud, let's see if we can find your car."

Transiting the towering pile-up, they walked deeper into the labyrinth of murdered automobiles. Uchoa had her head on a swivel, muttering as she walked, "That's the Rivian, and the Tesla, those five shitty Buicks, Subaru, Subaru, Subaru. Shit, where did they put the Civics? Oh, wait, I know."

They turned a corner, arriving at a dead end, surrounded by fifteen feet of stacked cars. The only way out was the way they'd come in. "Ah," Uchoa said. "Here it is. Civics. That your car, there?"

The wheelless Honda lay on a bed of broken glass and twisted door trim. Henry's heart sank. "No. That's black, and a...a later model. Mine is midnight blue. 1998. Listen, I got stuff to trade. I really need—"

Bruce nudged him hard from behind. "Are you sure? Midnight blue or black, aren't they the same thing?"

"No," Henry said. "No, they are not."

Uchoa rummaged in her coverall pockets and then held up a pair of rusty handcuffs. "Want to see a magic trick, Henry?" she asked brightly. "These are magician's cuffs. It's super cool, you'll see. Put them on."

Henry backed up, stumbling over his own feet. "What? Um, no, I'm good. Just looking for my car. If it's not here, I'll be on my way, thanks."

Uchoa tossed the handcuffs into the dirt. "Hard to believe you're this stupid. Typical normie entitlement. Coming out here with your 'Oh, let's have a civilized conversation! We're all rational, community-oriented people, right?' Well, guess what? No, we fuckin' ain't."

"Yeah, unfortunately, you going home is not gonna work for us, bud." His filed teeth bared in a snarl, Bruce pointed a cocked revolver at Henry's face. "We'll be needing you to stay here for a little while longer."

ELEVEN

THE SUN COMES AND goes, then comes and goes again. Dorothea feels these changes through the warming and cooling of the earth in which the tendrils rest. As time passes, the babble of voices, once so disorienting, begins to form into coherent patterns. Each voice, she realizes, tells its own story: fragments of lives lived, some mad, some sober, others wildly exuberant in their new, unimaginable, intangible forms. They tell of children, spouses, art, jobs. War. God and religion. Hatred, and love gone wrong. Like her, these disembodied voices were once people. People burned alive by the same monsters that murdered her. They should all be dead, and perhaps they are, but somehow, they aren't. They've all ended up *here*, ephemeral beings, ghosts left to haunt this...this in-between state. Wherever, and whatever that is.

Beyond these mysteries, she often thinks about Errol, and what went wrong between them. She knew he was working some angle with people living out on the waste ground, they'd already seen a fair bit of money from it, but he'd always been vague about the details. They'd fought in the past, sometimes physically, but never in a million years could she imagine he would resort to murder. Because even if he didn't do it himself, he *was* responsible for her death. Had he found out about the night she spent with Billy Pizarelli? She was no angel, but Errol had "slipped up" many times himself. Could be, he was just tired of her and wanted all that sweet waste ground money for his own.

After a time, she discovers her voice and begins to ask questions, reaching out to the others through an unspooling awareness, thinking the words through the network—but no one answers back. Up and down, up and down the highway of tendrils she flies, feeling everything occurring above and below. Frustrated, she screams her questions and makes accusations, demanding the attention of this strange *situation*, this closed system she now finds herself captive within. The memory of being set alight by her mysterious captors, the fiery agony, and the blessed relief of death, or what she thought was death, is still fresh in her mind. Why isn't she dead? Why this unknowing, this torture? Or, perhaps she is dead, and this is Hell... or purgatory? A purgatory created by Regina's god. The god of suffering and misery. That would make more sense.

Traveling to the edge of the network and then back to her point of origin, Dorothea soon realizes the circular nature of her prison.

The tendrils are formed into a spiral shape, one that trends inwards, ultimately leading to a center point. Curious, she follows the path, pushing deeper, traveling away from the babble of voices at the edges, into a strange and eerie silence.

Here, closer to the center, it begins to make sense that these lost souls are, like herself, trying to communicate with the collective awareness, but aren't an integral part of the Spiral. Making the connection, she realizes this must have something to do with the Cavity and her sacrifice. The...Kolchaks, had the old man called them? Wasn't that some corny old TV show? They were feeding and trying to communicate without the slightest understanding of what lay beneath their feet.

"We beseech thee, oh gods within the earth, the Cavity that shall engulf the wicked world, tell us your will, reveal to us your plan."

Dorothea feels the warmth of the Kolchak in the soil, she tastes the musky oils of exposed human flesh as it leeches into the sensitive surface tendrils, relaying sense imagery to the collective below. Do they kneel? Blood and gasoline on their praying hands? If only she could reach up and pull them down, underground, suffocate them, like a grave ghoul... She tries to respond, calling out curses, but without a larynx, without a tongue, the petitioner is deaf to her anger.

The next thing that strikes her is...*why*? If all the voices she hears are mute ghosts trapped in a prison of tendrils, why would this person pray to them? How did they know she and the others even existed? There is more to the mystery, but she moves on, traveling deeper, with the sense that answers might lie at the center of the Spiral.

TWELVE

THE DREADLOCKED WOMAN KEPT watch as Errol dragged Janelle from the Candy Wagon to the white paneled van. He moved fast, throwing her inside, onto a stained mattress, the smelly gag pulled tight across her face. Unlocking one of the cuffs, he reattached it to a second pair hanging from a crossbar, then sat back on the bumper breathing heavily.

"All set, Janny-girl," he said. "Trussed up like a pretty piglet and off to market. You'll like it with the Kolchaks, they know how to party like it's *1999*."

Janelle yanked off the gag with her free hand. "Fuck you."

The dreadlocked woman poked her head around the van. "Get out of there, unless you're comin' with."

Errol slid out. "You got what's mine?"

"'Course."

69

She pulled a taped-up envelope from the pocket of her coveralls and handed it over.

Errol opened it and fingered the wad of bills inside. "Nice."

"We need more. Many as you can get. You know how to reach me. Call, and I'll be right out."

Errol swept back his hair and saluted. "I'm on a duck hunt! See ya 'round, Janny." He waved and was gone.

The dreadlocked woman reached inside the van to check that the handcuff was secured, and Janelle kicked her, striking hard on the woman's thick hip. "Help! Somebody help me! Help! Call the police!"

The woman grunted, then crawled inside, closing the van door behind her. First, she held Janelle's legs, then she grabbed her free arm and twisted. Janelle cried out, hot tears springing into her eyes.

"Oh, kickin' me was a big mistake," the woman said. "You have no idea who I am, little girl. I don't cotton to disrespect."

Janelle struggled to free her hand. "Let me go right now, and I won't tell the cops."

The woman laughed and crawled atop Janelle, pinning her down. Oily, shapeless, dreads brushed her face as she struggled. "Get off me, bitch!"

The woman pulled a boxcutter from her back pocket, extending the blade with her thumb. "Hush, lie still now, little bird."

Janelle's blood ran cold. "What the fuck! Help! Somebody help me!"

Holding Janelle's arm in a vice-like grip, the woman quickly made a series of shallow cuts in the skin of her shoulder. Janelle thrashed and howled, tears springing to her eyes, but no matter how hard she tried, she couldn't budge her attacker. The woman bowed her head and began to lick the wounds, all the while grinding her hips against Janelle's legs. She'd put away the knife, her hand now down the front of her filthy jeans. The woman made small moans and grunts, lapping at the weeping cuts. "Mmm." She pushed her bloody lips close to Janelle's, kissing, and nuzzling her neck. "Oh, you taste so sweet, baby. Clean and fresh. Makes me so hot."

Once the woman had satisfied herself, she climbed off Janelle and exited via the back door. The van's engine grumbled to life. Beaten, bruised, Janelle tugged at the cuffs, but the steel ribs of the van's wall held firm. She fell back exhausted, the fresh cuts on her arm throbbing. She shuddered, still feeling the woman's horrible lips and tongue on her skin. In the end, she'd had no choice but to lie there and endure the nauseating assault. She was angry but also grateful it hadn't gone further. It could have been much worse. Bracing her legs against the wall, she pulled as hard as possible on the cuffs. "Aaaahhh!" The bar wouldn't give. She kicked the wall. "Fucking bitch!"

The van sped up, on the highway maybe—but to where?

A police siren sounded behind the van, and they eventually rolled to a stop. Janelle's heart raced. She would tell the cops about

Dorothea, tell them how Errol and this woman had kidnapped and assaulted her. Maybe there were other victims she could save.

Boots crunched in the gravel. Janelle hammered her feet on the side of the van, screaming at the top of her lungs. "Help! Help me!"

A male voice—*Cop?*—chuckled. "Whoa, what you hauling back there, Andrea? Sounds a little upset."

"Buncha goats," the dreadlocked woman replied, bored. "We're gonna start selling their milk at farmer's markets around town."

"Ooo, now that's a plan. Drink Kolchak Unpasteurized Goat's Milk! Won't kill you—not right away, at least."

"Funny guy."

Janelle hammered the wall, whimpering in frustration. What was with this cop?

"You know where the envelope is?" the policeman asked. "It's due today and we don't want to drive out there again."

"Viktor handles that. You gotta talk to him. Isn't the drop at Broughton?"

"Yeah, we looked there, but no dice. Would be a shame if we had to go all the way out to the Pile Up and...you know, begin an investigation."

"I'm sure it'll be there today. I'll tell Viktor to take care of it as soon as I see him."

"He better. Miss one time and the suggested donation doubles. Tell him that, too."

"I will."

The van's wall reverberated with Janelle's blows. "Fuck! Help me! I'm being kidnapped! Help!"

"Funny how goats sometimes sound eerily like people, isn't it?" the policeman remarked.

The van started up. "Yep. Just one of those crazy things. You have yourself a good day, officer."

THIRTEEN

HENRY RAISED HIS HANDS. "I got nothin', man. No cash, no car, and this fucking Android phone is four years old already. See?" He held his cell so Bruce could see. "The screen is even cracked."

"Shut up. Fuck your phone." Bruce swatted at it with the barrel of the pistol, all prior affability gone. "Put your stupid hands behind your back so Uchoa can get the cuffs on."

Henry did as he was told. Fear churned his insides. Bruce confiscated his phone, and after roughly patting him down, found the bag of weed. He stuck his nose inside the Ziplock, inhaling deeply. "Will you look at that, kid wasn't lying. Some really good shit there. Thanks, man."

Henry sighed. "Come on, dude. That's all I got, and honestly, it's not even mine. What are you guys gonna do to me?"

"I said, shut up." Bruce turned to the woman called Rhoda. "We can take him straight to the amphitheater."

Rhoda nodded. "March, *dude*." She leaned the long pole over her shoulder. "We got a lot of other shit to get done today."

The graveyard of stripped automobiles extended further than Henry had imagined, an overgrown labyrinth infested with a shocking number of feral dogs and cats. Twice, Rhoda used her forked spear to drive them away while Bruce, who had informed Henry his last name was Banner, of all things, kept the pistol trained on him. English ivy tripped the trio up on the narrow path, and a riot of blackberry canes tore at their clothing. Once driven off, the dogs would retreat into the sprawling blackberry thickets, barking wildly from behind their protective tangles of thorn.

Rounding a faded yellow Portland Public School bus hung with drying laundry, they entered an area of packed dirt, roughly oval, and surrounded by stripped cars. The ground here was scorched black, with numerous burned tires strewn about. A waterlogged mattress lay in the weeds along with a coffee maker and broken turntable. A man with long, stringy gray hair limped toward them. He was wearing a leg brace.

"What's this?" he asked. Henry saw that one of his hands was wrapped in a fresh, blood-stained bandage.

"Caught our friend here sneaking over by Camelot," Bruce Banner said. "We still got space in the cages?"

Leg Brace grimaced, hooking a gnarly, gray thumbnail. "Number four is empty. Don't put him in five. That weird church lady Bailey Jean brought in has lost it. She's full homicidal, yellin' about

Hell, and demons, and murder. Ready to bite balls." He cast a watery eye over Henry. "Judging on looks alone, this one ain't much of a fighter."

"What the fuck do you know?" Henry muttered under his breath.

Rhoda gripped his shoulder. "*Language.* Come on. March."

Henry bowed his head, following meekly until she released him. He waited about thirty seconds, drifting away slightly, and then took off running. Bruce Banner cursed. There were sounds of pursuit: feet slapping behind him, but he didn't look back. Running while wearing cuffs was much harder than he imagined, and after a few yards, the forward momentum tipped him into the dirt, face first. He rolled to a stop at the edge of a ditch, spitting dirt and gravel.

Rhoda, stronger than she looked, grabbed him by the scruff and hauled him to his feet. "All right, enough of that."

The ditch wasn't a ditch, but a hole. A strange, crusty hole in the ground with what looked like the shiny lid of a grand piano embedded in the dirt. Henry locked his knees, digging in. "What's that thing?"

Rhoda tugged hard on his arm. "Never mind, now. Nothing for you to be concerned about."

The piano lid lifted from the dirt, revealing a tangled mass of brown, moist roots, then clapped shut with a resounding *clack*, like a giant clamshell. Henry jumped. "What the fuck *is* that?"

This thing, this *creature,* was like nothing he had ever laid eyes on before. In the brief instant it was open, he'd glimpsed what looked like a leathery black gullet, muscular and glistening. The massive clamshell was glossy and chitinous, like the carapace of a beetle. It opened again, just a few inches, and a fetid, steaming cloud poured out. Moist compost and dead rat. Rancid vinegar. Henry gagged.

Bruce Banner jammed the pistol into his crotch. "Get moving," he growled. "I'm not having any more of this goofy bullshit. I swear, I'll gladly blow your fucking balls off right now."

Rhoda and Bruce frog-marched Henry to one of a half-dozen cages located behind a battered aluminum shed and locked him inside. Made from rebar, barbed wire, and pallet wood, the cages looked like a mental patient's DIY building project. A few were listing so badly they appeared in danger of imminent collapse. A nude woman in the adjacent cage shrieked and threw herself against the bars, clawing wildly, black orbs for eyes, her skin criss-crossed with angry red welts. Henry retreated to the far corner, where he saw that the other cages were filled with captives, a dozen or more slumped forms. Most looked like vagrants or drug addicts, not far off from the Kolchak's themselves.

"Put your arms close to the bars," Bruce Banner ordered. He removed the cuffs.

Henry massaged his wrists. "Listen, man. Hey, I don't know what this is, but if it's money you guys need, I can get it. Take me to an ATM. I'll give you everything I got."

Rhoda and Bruce Banner were already walking away. He rattled the rusted bars of the cage as the reality of what was happening bunched his gut into knots. "Hey! Please don't leave me in here!" he begged, almost sobbing. "You can keep my car! I'm sorry I trespassed! I swear, I'll give you everything!"

The nude woman screamed, a throat-shredding animal shriek, and thrashed against the walls of her confinement. "I'll kill you! I swear to the Lord Almighty, I will send each and every one of you to Hell!"

Henry dropped to his knees, head in his hands. "Well...shit. Shit, fuck, shit, fuckin' god damn, shit."

FOURTEEN

DOROTHEA SLOWS, THEN STOPS, testing the reach of her senses.

The babbling of the dead grows fainter the further she travels into the Spiral, replaced instead by a terrifying silence. There is something ahead, something lying in wait at the center, like a spider in its web. It presents as a void, currently incomprehensible, but it *is* something—something *alive*.

Has this void become quiet in response to her arrival? Judging her intentions just as she is now judging it? She presses on, circling closer, driven by curiosity. She isn't afraid, whatever it is. There isn't anything it can do to hurt her, considering she's already dead. The spirals become smaller and tighter as she nears the center, and soon she feels it, a *thump, thump, thump*, like the beating of some colossal heart. The sound radiates outward in all directions, through the moist tendrils, roots, earth, and stone, synching with every aspect of the complex network.

I feel you close—what are you, silver thing?

The words come through in much the same way she "feels" the animals, the birds, the insects, and the prayers of the living. A series of impressions somehow translated into meaning.

"I'm...Dorothea. I don't know why I'm here. I think I'm dead. Who are you?"

Aaaaaggggggaaaaaaaaahhhhhhh.

It is less a name and more an experience—an exhalation of vague images: immense distance, vast, unending darkness, mountains of jagged ice.

Why do you come to haunt aaaaaggggggaaaaaaaaahhhhhhh, silver thing?

"Maybe I'm a ghost, but I don't know where I am, or how I got here. I don't mean to haunt you. They burned me... The people, those people up there. I—I don't wanna remember any of that..."

Part of us now, silver thing. To grow, to live, to prosper—to eat.

Eat? This is not the afterlife Dorothea had imagined.

"What is it you want from me?"

The response is overwhelming, a cascading sensory overload: *hungryhungryhungryhungryhungryhungryhungryhungryhungryhungryhungryhungryhungry.*

FIFTEEN

Janelle turned her head, blinded by sunlight streaming into the back of the van.

"All right," the dreadlocked woman said, a retractable metal baton held at her side. "Gonna unhook you from the wall. Fight or kick me, and I'll beat your ass senseless. Hear?"

Janelle could see trees. A lot of them. The van had left the highway, traveling slowly over bumpy ground for quite some distance. They could be anywhere. The woman relocked the cuffs with her arms in front, which was a relief, and then helped her out of the van. Yellow sunlight pierced the clouds to the west, but here it was still drizzling, tiny, wet diamonds flung sideways by the steady wind.

They walked together through a pine forest strewn with trash, the dreadlocked woman holding onto her arm so she couldn't run away. When they reached a forked and muddy path, the woman kept her eyes on the trees ahead, as if she were expecting someone.

Janelle realized she'd overplayed the tough girl, on-the-fly detective bit. The cops being in on it or bought off brought everything into sharp focus. Through Errol, Dorothea had fallen in with very bad people, and they weren't playing games. They were both in serious trouble.

"What are you going to do to me?"

The woman shook her head. "Nothing from me, baby girl. So, don't be afraid. I had mine." She snickered. "You're gonna be part of our family soon. The Kolchaks are giving you a gift, one that will be written about in history books. Right place, right time, right temperature. We're all pioneers working on a brave new frontier, an organic singularity."

She tested the woman's vice-like grip. *But where would I run? Where is safe?* "I don't know what any of that means."

Two people appeared on the path, a buxom woman carrying a long pole and a child. The dreadlocked woman waved. "Hey."

Now that they were close, Janelle saw it wasn't a child at all, but a little person, an adult man with a wispy mustache and dark eyes. He wore new tennis shoes and had a gun tucked in his waistband. Frown lines creased his forehead.

"Fuck. Another one?" he said. "At this rate, we're never gonna get to eat lunch."

"This your catch?" Aside from the weird, forked stick, the woman looked like any other Portland white woman, an ex-hippy with long graying braids wearing blue jean overalls and a stained pink tank top.

"Nah. She came from that creepy, rockabilly dirtbag. He called it in on the hotline."

"That pig needs to go to the feast, too," Bruce Banner said. "I don't know why we fraternize with such lowlifes."

The dreadlocked woman shrugged. "He brings in warm bodies, and that's what Bailey Jean wants. I don't question, and neither should y'all."

"I'm not questioning," the man insisted. "Just sayin'."

"Have either of you seen Viktor? I got pulled over by one of our pig friends. He claimed Viktor hasn't made this week's drop."

The overall woman shook her head. "No, not since last night."

"Shit. If you see him, tell him about the cops. It's important," the dreadlocked woman said. "I have to go back out and run some errands."

Janelle was prodded down the muddy path by her two captors. Homeless camps were nothing new to her, she'd experienced a few in Florida, but this one was especially dire. In addition to the usual scene of wilted tents moldering in tangled nests of cast-off household goods, there were also dead animals lying everywhere. Desiccated, stiffened corpses and heaps of gristle-snarled bones tucked in among ruined nature, peeking out from under the hillocks of rotting rubbish, or piled haphazardly at the foot of trees. Crows hopped and squawked in the glittering fields of broken glass, fighting over the remains. Janelle averted her eyes, trying to breathe through her mouth.

Along the path lay a fenced graveyard. Crooked wooden crosses and cut-up plastic slabs, makeshift markers stuck in the dirt of over two dozen man-and-animal-sized mounds. The whole place stank of rot and death.

"My name is Janelle." She addressed the female captor, desperate to make any kind of friendly connection. "What's yours?" The woman's freckled forearm bore a tattooed heart emblazoned with the words: MY BUDDY.

"Shut up." Bruce Banner nudged her in the back. "No talking."

Piles of cars began where the tree line ended—stolen, Janelle assumed—hoods open, windows smashed, tires missing. Behind a campervan with four flat tires, a pair of teenagers squatted around a sputtering campfire passing a paper bag. Empty spray paint cans littered the ground. One of the teens swayed to his feet.

"Heya, Rhoda." He waved, scratching at a dirty bandage on his head. He was still young, but the drugs had prematurely aged him, the jeans hanging from his waist tattered to the point of nonexistence, showing more bare, filthy skin than denim. "You guys got a cigarette?"

The woman, Rhoda, took a crumpled pack from her coveralls and handed it to him. The boy lit up as if his life depended on it, dragging deep. "You goin' all the way tonight?" Rhoda asked.

The teen nodded, pushing long, greasy hair from his eyes. "Fuck yeah. I'm thinkin' the whole leg this time." He hopped, lifting a rotten sneaker, and nearly fell. "Shit's gonna be epic, I know it." He pumped his fist into the air. "Kolchaks, muthafukas! Don't ever fuck with us! We feast!"

"Good boy," Rhoda said. "Shit *will* be epic, I promise you."

"Listen, I'm fucking on the verge of, no, way *past* hangry," Bruce Banner said. "Can we dump this bitch and get on with it?"

More wrecked cars and a lineup of tiny shacks lay on the far side of the teenage huffer's camp. Dragged forward, Janelle realized these shacks were *cages*, makeshift enclosures of welded rebar and razor wire with multiple prisoners locked inside. Hope flared anew. Maybe her sister was here.

"Dorothea!" she called out, voice more a hoarse croak than a shout. "Dorothea, it's Janelle! Where are you? *Dorothea!*"

No one answered.

"Put her in six," Bruce Banner ordered.

The cage door was secured by a combination lock, and the woman uncuffed Janelle before pushing her inside. A man crouched in the corner of the smelly cage—doughy, balding, early thirties maybe. He was flushed pink, and it looked like he'd been crying. With the door shut, only a few feet separated them.

He wiped his grimy face, sniffling. "Hey."

SIXTEEN

IN THE FUCKED-UP ANNALS of Henry's stupid, fucked up life, being locked in a cage by homeless meth heads while trying to retrieve his junker Honda, was certainly the lowest point by a longshot.

The lowest point so far, he thought, choking back a strangled laugh. The homeless meth heads probably had lots more bullshit planned. And once they realized there was no one willing to pay a ransom for his sorry ass...well, he hoped they'd at least show him pity or be merciful. He wasn't so far off from them, after all, and it wouldn't be the first time he'd been reduced to begging.

After an hour in the cage, Henry needed to urinate. He called out, kicking the bars, making a racket, trying to get attention, but no one responded. *And Digger,* he thought angrily, *where is he?* His supposed goddamn *best* friend. Where were the fucking cops? With all that was going on, kidnappings, drugs, there should have been two S.W.A.T teams out here by now. Henry vowed if he got out by himself, he'd smash Digger's favorite vape into a million pieces. Fantasizing Digger's stricken face made Henry feel a little better, but he still had to go. Badly.

"Hello! Hey!" he called out to the two Kolchaks nodding out on plastic folding chairs next to the aluminum shed.

"I have to pee! Hey! Can I go in the bushes, please?"

"Fuck, dude," said a man in the next closest cage. "What do you think this is? Scout camp? They're not letting any of us out. Shut up and piss in the corner already."

Neither of the Kolchaks stirred from their chairs, and Henry turned shamefacedly away from his neighbors to relieve himself through the bars. He didn't even want to imagine what would happen when he had to go number two. While he zipped up, Bruce Banner and Rhoda emerged from behind the aluminum shed with a handcuffed prisoner between them. Bruce Banner yapped orders, and they pushed the new captive, a young woman, into Henry's cage.

Henry greeted her, but she just stared at him, possibly in shock. She was dark-haired and moon-faced, Hispanic, and for a moment he considered that maybe she didn't speak any English.

She backed against the cage door. "Hello."

"Um. Yeah. I guess we're sharing?"

"Guess so."

"I'll stay on this side, so don't worry."

"Thank you."

The woman squatted in the far corner. He hadn't thought to ask her name, and now with the moment passed it seemed too awkward. Henry sighed and sat.

The sun was already lost behind the trees, shadows prematurely darkening the barren valley. More dark gray clouds bunched up on the horizon, threatening heavy rain. Once it got dark, Henry was certain he'd be able to find a way out of the cage. He imagined all the Kolchaks were like the ones in the folding chairs, at some point, they'd all be too drugged out to stop him from escaping.

"Why—" the woman said, fingers looped around the bars of the cage, perilously close to the rows of rusted razor wire. "What are they going to do with us? Will we be...ransomed? Killed?"

Henry wondered if she was about to lose it. Crying, screaming maybe. "I don't know. I'm new here, too. It'll be okay."

"What do they want?"

"I don't know. We just have to wait and see. Try and stay strong."

"Do you know a woman named Dorothea? Or maybe Dana? Looks a bit like me, but older. Longer hair. She was with a guy named Errol."

"No, why?"

"She's my sister. I'm looking for her."

"No, I'm sorry. We've never crossed paths. You think she's out here?"

"I-I don't know. I was abducted by that guy Errol I mentioned. He, uh, I have no idea, he *sold* me to these people, I guess? But I don't know for what reason. Do you know what a *Kolchak* is? Some, like, homeless...drug gang?"

"I'm sorry. There are so many shitty people in this town. They call themselves Kolchaks, after a TV show, or something. Or maybe it's a joke. A meme. All I know is we gotta get out of here. Escape somehow."

She grimaced. "You think we can?"

"We can try. What's your name? I'm Henry."

"Janelle."

He held out his hand and she grasped it, grateful for a friendly hand, even if it was shaking. "Let's see what we can get going after they all go to sleep."

As darkness fell, the Kolchaks lit torches and stoked the campfires. Most of their activity was centered around the ditch where Henry had seen the giant, shiny clam, or whatever it was. *Cavity*, he'd overheard them calling it, and imagined a decayed black hole in a tooth, only this cavity was much larger and in the ground. Something wrong, something rotted. How deep did the rot go? The Cavity opened and shut, clacking like a monster's maw—a hungry predator—alive and terrifying. His teeth ached in fearful sympathy, and he realized he was grinding them together.

The feral woman in the next cage moaned, scrabbling at the bars. The moaning grew louder, a gurgling hiss. Janelle sidled across the cage, and Henry made room for her on his side.

"I don't even want to know what that is," she whispered.

More Kolchaks arrived. At least twenty milled between the cages and the ditch. Dogs yipped and howled in the distance. Rhoda, Bruce Banner, and two men Henry hadn't seen before carried wooden pallets and sheets of plywood from the auto graveyard, then stacked them up, building what appeared to be a makeshift stage. The rainclouds had moved on, and a sliver of yellow moon was now hung in the sky. People drank like it was a house party, passing around cans of White Claw and bottles of fortified wine. A skinny teenage boy with a bandaged head, nude but for a pair of filthy, tattered briefs, mounted the rickety stage, raising his tattooed arms over his head. The crowd clapped and hooted. A woman carrying bolt cutters climbed up behind him, and he turned to embrace her.

"Bailey Jean! Bailey Jean! Bailey Jean!" the crowd chanted, stomping their feet.

The woman waved for quiet. She was petite, and well-dressed in comparison to the others, wearing an expensive Patagonia fleece and new hiking boots. "My children. We're close, oh so close! With every feast we prepare for the Cavity, with every tiny sacrifice y'all make, our little community comes that much closer to understanding secrets that have been hidden since the time of Atlantis. Together, we're decoding the future."

Janelle pressed her face to the bars. "Do you know what they're on about?"

Bailey Jean addressed the boy, holding the bolt cutters close to his face. "Kit? Are you prepared to embrace the next step in your journey?"

Kit swallowed hard, raising a trembling hand. "Yeah—um, Yes! I'm ready, I want to give everything."

Two Kolchaks held the boy steady as Bailey Jean centered the blades of the bolt cutter on his index finger. The cut was quick and decisive, and she immediately scooped up the fallen appendage, throwing it in the ditch. Blood flowed from the stump, trickling down Kit's forearm. But Bailey Jean didn't stop there: one, two, three, four, the rest of the boy's fingers were amputated in quick succession, falling with faint thuds onto the plywood stage. Henry heard multiple loud *clackings* as the cryptid opened and closed.

A painful, high-pitched squeal filled the air, and everyone but Kit rushed to cover their ears. It seemed to have come from the Cavity, but Henry recognized it as the same sound that had driven off the feral dog pack.

Bailey Jean grasped the boy's shoulders. "Kit! Quickly! What is it you see?" When he didn't respond, she slapped his face. "Kit! Tell us what you see!"

"I-I." Kit wobbled, blood dripping from the stump of his hand. "I see—a billion stars, and the lights of a great, a great city, it...it covers...the whole...the whole world. The Lord Jesus is there. On a throne. With a host of ang—angels at his back. And the people—the people there are...screaming...oh my god...they're screaming, burning, all on fire. Children, everyone, oh, they're dying... I smell the burning flesh... They've been turned to ash...but, but... Shit... All it's doing is making me hungry...so, so hungry... Like cooked steak. A roast. I'm on fire, too..."

Kit's eyes rolled and he fell backward, his head bouncing from the plywood stage. Kolchaks rushed to his side, carrying him off into the darkness.

"What the fuck?" Janelle muttered.

"A vision of the future!" Bailey Jean crowed. "The end of this wicked world, mankind devoured by the Cavity in preparation for the return of Christ! Now, who's next? Who will make us an even greater sacrifice?"

A figure stepped from the shadows. "I will. Take my leg. I find it does me no good where it is."

Torches drew closer and Henry saw it was the mechanic who had spoken, the one who lied and placed him in cuffs. She wobbled like she was drunk.

Bailey Jean seemed to hesitate. "Uchoa. Are you certain of this? You've already given once."

Uchoa exposed her stump. "I gave my hand to the Cavity, and it spoke to me, showed me things I would have never dreamed possible. But now that it's healed, the visions grow fuzzy and distant. I need more. *It* needs more—of me. Bring the saws so that I might give further of myself, I'm anxious to begin."

"So be it." Bailey Jean raised a hand. "Rhoda! Where are you?"

"I'm here." Rhoda handed off a torch. "My kit is on the bus. She'll need a tourniquet and an epidural. Uchoa, from the knee joint, right?"

"That'll do for now." The mechanic nodded "Thank you, Rhoda."

Henry watched, mesmerized, as Uchoa lay down on a tarp that had been draped across the stage, wearing only a pair of black boxers. Watched until Rhoda nodded at the two Kolchaks restraining Uchoa's arms and positioned the rust-speckled bone saw on the woman's antiseptic-painted knee. After that, he turned his face away, jamming his fingers in his ears to blot out the wet sawing noises and terrible screams.

Janelle touched his arm, and he recoiled. "Are you okay?"

Henry pressed himself against the bars of his cage. "It's all gonna be fine. Right? It's all gonna be fine. Everything will work out...just fine. Right?"

SEVENTEEN

"HAVE YOU ALWAYS... LIVED here?"

No.

"Then where?"

We come up from the endless dark, silver thing. We traverse the frozen void from grains of sand...to mountains...to worlds... No gulf is too large, too small... No light too bright...or too cold...

Dorothea spends time engaging with *aaaaagggg-ggaaaaaaaaahhhhhhh* but the entity offers few real answers. As far as sentience goes, it seems quite limited, and much of what it does say makes little sense. *Hungry. Eat. Cold. Silver thing.* This last one is a mystery. Can it "see" her? And if so, why does she appear silver? Is she a light? Heat? Energy? Despite talking in circles, she still isn't any closer to discovering what the thing is or why she's ended up here.

Unsure what to do next, Dorothea pushes her awareness through the network of root fibers connecting—*Aaaaagggg-ggaaaaaaaaahhhhhhh*—to the world around it. At the edges of the Spiral, voices still chatter and rage. One stands out from the incessant din, and unsure of why that is, she homes in on it.

"Come to me, O Lord of the earth," the voice pleads. "I gave myself willingly to y'all, a guest at your great feast, offering the ultimate sacrifice. Why do you deny me, O Lord? Take my soul from this cold, dark purgatory and deliver it unto the Heaven we was all promised. Amen."

Hearing him brings it all back. It's the old man who perished alongside her. The one who eagerly accepted the flames and tried to convince her to do the same. The last person she spoke with before the end. She expands her awareness, calling out to him much like she's done with the hungry thing at the center of the Spiral, and surprisingly, the man responds.

"Lord? Hast thou come to take a wretched, lonely soul?"

Dorothea decides to play along. "I have."

"You're a silver light, Lord, a shining beacon in the abyss. My heart is gladdened."

There it is again. Silver. For him, and the others, she sees nothing, only feels their voices. Why do they see her differently?

"I waited, Lord. And I sent my mouse in search of you. When will you take me? When will I see Paradise? Now, Lord?"

"Soon, my child. Soon," she answers. "What is your mouse? One of the rodents in the forest above us?"

"No. Haven't you seen them, my Lord? I call it a mouse, but I don't know what it is. Mice grow at the surface, bunching where the roots curl tight. It runs for me, and through it, I see the world we left behind."

"You make these things?"

"No. They make themselves, Lord. The mice sleep in the roots of the trees, and I use them to look back, to remember what was good about my life. Courtesy of your divine creation, of course."

"Of course."

"Am I going to Paradise, Lord? Soon?"

"You are. But I need you to be patient."

"I'm patient, Lord. Here until you call me."

Rising through the root network to the trees, Dorothea senses the places where the fine hairs have indeed bunched into clumps. As if attuned to her presence, the hairs grow, pushing through the soil, then twine together to form a fragile, hollow sphere. The sphere then pushes up and away from the tangle of roots and emerges on the surface. Images begin to appear to Dorothea: green, bowing leaves, holly, and fern.

But how? How is this possible?

With a bit of effort, she finds she can change the angle of view. Branches, leaf litter, the wrinkled brown bark of a towering fir bole. Breaking free, the mouse rolls along the forest floor like a miniature tumbleweed. There is more: a sliver of blue sky. Clouds. She laughs in delight, which in time turns to weeping.

"Do you see the past, my Lord? Where the living still breathe? Where we suffered, and died? They eat, Lord, but I'm still hungry, starvin' for salvation."

It takes all of Dorothea's will to tear her attention from the visions of the rolling mouse. "I see it now, my child. Thank you. But it's true, you've suffered much too long. Let's see what we can do about getting you fed."

EIGHTEEN

JANELLE RETCHED, COVERING HER face with her hands.

These freaks were *sacrificing* themselves. Well, bits of themselves. A finger here, an ear there—a leg. Throwing bloody offerings to something living in a trash-filled ditch in a place no one could be bothered to even evict them from. Madness.

"I'm pretty sure we're next," Henry said, deep in shadow. "Why else would they keep us here?"

She shifted on the hard ground. One of her legs had fallen asleep. Someone close by was sobbing, possibly in one of the other cages, it was hard to tell. "What can we do?"

"Well...these cages are junk, thrown together. Besides the razor wire, they're only rebar, two-by-fours, and zip ties. When the weirdos pass out, I think the two of us could make a big enough hole to squeeze through."

In the flickering firelight, four Kolchaks loaded Uchoa onto a gurney, her fresh stump swathed in blood-stained bandages. The other woman, the leader, stood at the victim's side, holding her hand. Uchoa pulled the leader down and whispered in her ear. When she was finished, the leader raised her hand for quiet. "Sister Uchoa has told me of her great vision, and now she will tell you!"

Uchoa raised up on one elbow. "I saw that the Lord is already among us!" Her voice was hoarse and strained. "So close that we cannot see them! But our long wait is almost over! Within two days, the Lord will reveal themself to us, and we shall receive our final reward!"

A rising howl rippled across the mass of Kolchaks, and they began to dance around the creature in the ditch, singing and swinging their torches.

Ochoa fell back on the gurney and the leader whooped, pumping her fist. "We are Kolchaks, the terrors of the night!"

Janelle sank into the dirt, rear-end chilled, arms wrapped around her knees. All at once the grief poured out, hot tears leaking from her eyes.

Dorothea was dead. Errol, with the help of these people, had killed her.

A sob escaped her lips.

"Hey," Henry whispered. "Listen. We'll get out, okay?" There was a quaver in his voice—he didn't believe his own words. Yet, Janelle needed them to be true.

"I know." She rubbed her face, sniffling. "We can do this."

"But it's okay to cry, too. I did already."

After the divorce, Momma moved them to Tampa when Janelle was eleven and Dorothea fourteen. The Queen's confidence had been thoroughly wrecked by her husband's infidelity and subsequent accidental death. She was certain this was a test from God. Stewing in the rented aquamarine ranch house, Regina soon spiraled from Virginia Slims and glasses of red wine to hard liquor and Xanax. When wasted enough, she would scream and rage at the sisters, her captive audience of two. Dorothea always took the brunt of it, pushing back, shielding Janelle from their mother's wrath. Janelle and Dorothea grew to be inseparable. Sisters bound by love and the vagaries of a shared trauma experience. When they were together, laughing, in, or out of trouble, Janelle convinced herself nothing the world had to offer could ever tear them apart.

Then Dorothea met Mat.

Mat was your typical high school skater, with a floppy fringe of auburn hair and busted-up red high-top Vans. Sagging jeans on skinny hips and a ridiculous chain wallet. Now almost sixteen, Dorothea fell hard, and at her new boyfriend's urging, fell into the same sort of things she'd spent years hating Regina for. Then she got pregnant, and Mat decided he was going to drop out of high school to take a job on his brother's fishing boat. Handing Dorothea two hundred dollars in cash for the abortion, he left early the next morning. Janelle sat in a car outside of Planned

Parenthood, reading Percy Jackson as a neighbor lady—a local activist and community organizer named Lil—escorted Dorothea to the procedure. Thankfully for them all, Regina never got wind. Her sister came out pale and drawn, skin painted with pink streaks. In the days and weeks that followed, Dorothea pined for Mat, and mourned her baby, spiraling further into bouts of depression and drinking.

Fast forward a year, and Dorothea was dating another dumb ass skater who soon admitted he was bi and cheating on her with one of his male cousins. More feckless boys came and went in a haze of weed smoke and Natural Light. Janelle could remember some of their names: Jamal, Cody, Bogs, Kaden, but the faces were all a blur. Meanwhile, Regina rediscovered God, got clean, and then got mean. Mean*er*. Drunk or sober though, the "ungrateful" daughters would always be the target of her angry fits.

Janelle tried to be protective, as Dorothea had done with her. For a long time, she played the role of supportive wing woman, hair-holding as her sister puked her guts out, fetching burritos and Cokes at midnight, distracting Regina when Dorothea wanted to sneak out past curfew. Boys didn't interest Janelle, but neither did girls and when it came to sex or romance, she couldn't see the point. Much too complicated. Too much effort. Books, friends, and video games were all she needed.

Not so for Dorothea though, who was out there proactively *looking* for something.

Anything.

Then came Errol.

"Hey. I think the last finally one conked out," Henry whispered. "I've been working on these ties."

"What do you need me to do?"

"Feel around for weak spots. Find places where the ties are slack, or the wood is rotten. Watch your fingers, though. The razor wire is rusty but still sharp."

Janelle did as he instructed, feeling blindly at the junctures of rebar and wood, pulling at the zip ties until she found one that was broken. She snapped a second tie by levering the rebar, then a third, pulling hard on the chill, moist metal. Soon, she could stick her hand out of the cage, but without being able to make a larger hole there was no way to safely crawl out. It was too dark to see what Henry was doing. She could hear him work, scratching and pulling at the walls of their prison.

"Any luck?" she asked.

"I'm trying to bend the razor wire without cutting myself but it's hard." He sounded flustered. "You?"

Pulling at the razor wire, spikes of pain shooting through her fingers and palms as she gripped tight, Janelle clenched her jaw and kept tugging. Pain be damned, she thought, even as blood spilled to the dirty soil beneath her. The twisted, jagged metal of the razor dug into her—she felt it scraping insider her, hungry for bone and cartilage.

She bit her lips, pulled her lips tight, stifling the screams building inside her. *Nobody can hear me*, she thought. *Don't let them hear me.*

Finally, with blood spilling down her forearms, pooling at her knees, she said, "I made enough room for my hand, but I'm having the same problem as you."

Henry's shadow rose from the floor. "You know, maybe there's a weakness where the lock holds the door. Let me take a look."

Errol and Dorothea met through her part-time job at HH-Gregg. She worked at the South Tampa location in the appliances department. He was the store manager. Errol Sanchez was a different man then, slick, well-dressed, with an almost-new Mercedes and a pastel condo on the water. He always arrived at Regina's house bearing little gifts, bought take-out, flattered, and fawned, talked about God and family. Prosperity. Republican and Christian grift. Sure, he was a little bit older, but that's exactly what Regina felt Dorothea needed in her life. A strong male presence to guide her into adulthood. Motherhood. Even Janelle had been fooled. At first. Within six months, Errol popped the question and put an adequate ring on it. The Queen was ecstatic. God had answered her prayers.

Janelle was surprised but not shocked the first time she walked in on her sister and brother-in-law doing meth. Something strange had been going on for a while. After that, it was all downhill. By the time Regina cut them off completely, Dorothea and Errol were full-blown addicts.

"Fuck." Henry's shadow sank into the corner. "There's no way we can do this without tools." Janelle heard a sucking sound. "My hand is bleeding," he said. "I better not get fucking tetanus, on top of it."

She made an exasperated noise. "I don't think you need to worry about that right now."

"*Hey*." Both jumped. A voice whispered from outside the cage. "*Henry*."

"Is that you? Jesus, dude, it's about time."

"Shut up. I'm getting you out."

Janelle couldn't see the man's face. "Do you know this person?"

"Yeah, he's my friend. We came here together but got separated. He ran away."

"Can you both keep quiet," Digger hissed. "I found a fucking hammer, but this is gonna take a minute."

NINETEEN

WITH ALL THE NOISE Digger was making and the swearing under his breath, Henry was shocked no Kolchaks had come round to investigate. It probably helped that the crazy woman in the next cage started screaming and moaning and scratching again—not even a cabal of drugged-out cultists wanted to deal with that mess.

Using the hammer, Digger was able to make a hole in the razor wire big enough for Henry and Janelle to slither through, and once they were free, they crouched low among the cars, running for the safety of the tree line. Paranoid, and worried they were still making too much noise, Henry dropped on all fours and crawled inside the first lavender bush he encountered. Janelle and Digger followed, and they all crouched close in the leaves like a trio of frightened rabbits.

"Dude. It's like *Mad Max* around here," Digger whispered. "I was making a beeline for the road and a couple of fucking tweakers tried to jump me. I shot them both. Killed 'em. And look at this shit." Digger pulled a wrinkled envelope from his jacket. Inside was a large sum of money, a thick stack of crisp hundred-dollar bills. "One of the assholes I shot, a bald dickhead with tats and a beard, had this on him. Won't be needing it now, though." He said those last words with a devilish smile, which sent an unexpected shiver down Henry's spine.

It was either an exaggeration or an outright lie, but Henry let it go. "Oh, well booya for you, big hero. Never did find my car, and you left me to almost get killed, asshole. Why didn't you shoot those people that ran up on me?"

Digger peeked through the branches of the bush. The Kolchaks either hadn't realized they'd escaped or were too drugged to come after them. "Sorry, man. When I took off, I thought you were right behind me. I didn't look, I just booked it out of there. Listen, I'll split this cash with you, give you a third of it."

Henry snorted. "*Of course.* Split means half, you cretin. By the way, Digger, this is Janelle. We met in the cage."

"Cages, what the *fuck.* Jesus." Digger fed bullets into the cylinder of the .38.

Janelle nodded, face hidden in her long hair, but said nothing.

"Where'd you get more bullets?" Henry asked.

"My car. That's why it took me so long to find you, I needed ammo for the firefight. And thank God I got it." He snapped the cylinder shut. "Oh, and I also grabbed my spare key, in case something happens, and we get split up again."

Digger handed the key to Henry, who stared at it in disbelief. "You're giving me your fob?"

"Yeah, and don't lose it. If things go south, run, and then find the cops."

"The police won't come," Janelle mumbled. "The Kolchak that kidnapped me was talking to one of them when she brought me here. I screamed and he ignored me. They're all in it together."

Digger stared out into the darkness, still breathing heavily. "Fuckin' pigs. I shoulda known."

Someone shouted, and flashlight beams played across the line of cages. The Kolchaks who had fallen asleep in folding chairs or on the grass lurched to their feet, with more streaming from the tin shed. There were new arrivals, one of which carried an automatic rifle.

"Shit." Digger pushed the cash envelope into his coat pocket. "I think they figured out you're gone."

The Kolchaks with flashlights fanned out to search the area. Luckily, they were moving in the opposite direction from where the three lay hidden, but it was only a matter of time.

Digger tapped Henry on the shoulder. "We gotta go. We gotta go. We gotta go."

"Okay, but let's just wait a sec and see if they settle down. Run if they come this way. We're well hidden here."

Digger's jaw dropped, his eyes widening in disbelief. "Dude. I fuckin' can't believe it. The one with the flashlight on his AR, you see him? That's the asshole I took the money from."

"What? The bearded guy? I thought you said you killed him?"

"I did. I did, man. Not lyin'. He was dead, I checked."

"Well, he's not dead now."

"Let's go." Janelle insisted.

"There's packs of aggressive dogs in the trees," Henry said. "They attacked us, but something ran them off, like a high-pitched noise."

"So, we'll just stay here until they find us? They'll see us right away when the sun comes up."

"No. I don't know. Fuck."

"I agree with her." Digger said, nodding at Janelle. "I'd take my chances with the dogs over that walking-dead tweaker."

The flashlights had returned to the cages. The crazy woman gibbered, and Henry heard the meaty *thwacks* as she threw herself against the bars of the cage. The lights now turned in their direction, drawing closer.

Janelle stood up. "I'm going."

TWENTY

PILOTING THE MOUSE IS strange. Intoxicating. Dorothea floats unseen through the night forest, perceiving the world through a hollow, almost weightless ball of intertwined root fibers. The animals, the birds, anything living, glows in her sight, and she senses the life force pulsing within them, their fearful and furtive running. The humans whisper in their sleep, and she watches a pair fuck in a ditch, a singular mass of glowing, writhing limbs and breathless exclamations. The world is far different at ground level, slower, and more immediate. She feels the pull of the moon and the voice of a wind that seeks to scour everything from its path. In the throes of this odd death, this in-between place, she feels more alive than ever. No drugs, no cops, no Errol, no Regina. Or money, or work, or rent, or anything. This un-feeling is now her whole world.

Hungry.

The entity at the center of the Spiral communicates one thing and one thing only. Dorothea is a part of it, a reluctant participant in this inexplicable sense collective, with no way of shutting the message out. The thing broods on the outskirts of her awareness, a presence, and Dorothea assumes it must see her as little more than an intrusive flash, a rat scrabbling in the walls. But it does recognize her, it's aware she and the others exist, yet seems powerless to stop or evict them. Are they an infection? A virus? Or just an easily dismissible bout of indigestion? In the end, none of that matters, as all the entity desires is to *feed* and *grow*. Rain and sun must have been its early sustenance, then somewhere along the way, it evolved to consume flesh, developing a mouth with which to lie in wait for prey, like a gigantic Venus flytrap, eating the things that stumbled into its grasp, mindless, but localized. A rabbit here, a dog or deer there. Not much, at first.

Until the Kolchaks discovered it.

Dorothea's mouse reaches the amphitheater of gutted cars. This is where she perished, screaming, inhaling the stink of charred meat, and this too is where the Kolchaks fed her corpse to the Cavity.

But why?

That's the question. Why feed human flesh to some animal oddity living in a trash-filled ditch? What did they hope to gain? Was it just...a kind of insanity, a drug-fueled madness?

Dozens of sleeping human bodies shimmer in the darkness, identical to a dog or a deer, no different from the wriggling worms in the earth, just larger, brighter. Dorothea wonders which of them is the teenager who set her on fire. Revenge would be so nice. Maybe she could lure him into the Cavity, then torment his newbie consciousness once he joins the rest of the consumed...

The mouse is already disintegrating, the glass and trash she's rolled through taking its toll on the fragile root hairs. Dorothea senses its light fading. Up ahead, a dozen bodies lie close together on the cold ground. Upon closer inspection, she realizes they aren't cultists, but more victims locked inside cages.

Future sacrifices.

Red gas cans along the wall of a tin shed confirm her suspicions, and she feels a brief stab of pity for the imprisoned. They will be burned alive, or have their throats cut. Tossed into the voracious Cavity. The wilted, damaged mouse expires at the foot of one of the cages, returning Dorothea to the darkness below. But as it disintegrates, she hears two people whispering, and for a moment, she swears one of them sounds exactly like her sister.

Twenty-One

Janelle tapped softly at the door of the garden shed. The ancient tin shed lay nestled between two enormous azalea bushes, their flowers withered and brown. "Hey. You awake in there?" she whispered.

"Yeah," Dorothea replied from the other side of the flimsy plywood. A locked brass padlock hung from the latch, the key to which Regina kept on a silver chain around her neck along with her crucifix.

"Mom said she's going to let you out after supper. But you don't get any. I'll save you a biscuit if I can."

"Fuck her."

"Dorothea!"

"I don't care. God will understand. *She's* the evil one, not me."

Janelle didn't rise to the bait. It wasn't the first time her sister had talked that way about their mother. Sometimes she felt like a

117

soccer ball, trapped between two players, kicked back and forth by their constant struggle. It was exhausting. And when dealing with either, only one tactic seemed to work: change the subject.

"Marcy said she won't lend me her DVD, but we can watch it at her house if we want." Dorothea was obsessed with *Stuart Little*. She'd found out Janelle's rich friend Marcy had the new DVD and begged her to ask Marcy if they could borrow it. Regina hated *Stuart Little*, but that was no surprise. She hated all movies. And music. Anything popular these days was just more "Godless Hollywood" to her.

"For real?" The hinges creaked as Dorothea pressed on the door of the shed. "When?"

"Any weekend. You can sneak out. We'll put pillows under my covers, and I'll tell her you're sleeping in my bed with me."

"What about you? Don't you want to see it?"

"I'll see it after you."

Dorothea went quiet. Janelle thought she'd moved away from the door when she whispered, "I wish God hadn't called Daddy."

"Yeah."

"You don't even remember him anymore."

"I do! A little."

"What if God called me? Would you be sad at all?"

Janelle swallowed hard, tearing up. "Stop it. You know I'd cry and cry. Promise me you won't ever leave!"

Having received the desired reaction, Dorothea chuckled. "Don't worry, I'll always take care of my baby sis."

TWENTY-TWO

"Ow. Shit. This is fucked! Damn it!"

The taller, sporty-but-hippyish guy Henry had called "Digger," had lagged behind to look at something. Now he was limping and making faces. If it wasn't for their car, Janelle would have ditched both of them an hour ago. "What's wrong?"

Digger caught up, sucking air through gritted teeth. The grip of the .38 she'd seen him loading hung free from his swinging jacket pocket. "I think I stepped on a goddamned nail. There's so much shit on the ground out here. And I can't see a thing."

"Can you still walk?"

"Yeah, but we gotta go to urgent care when we get out of here. I need a shot, so I don't contract lockjaw or something."

Henry squinted in the direction they'd seen the flashlights. "We can slow down now. I don't see them."

Gingerly, Janelle stepped around the jagged, rusty edges of a crumpled trash can. "You're sure your car is this way?"

Digger shrugged. "I'm sure it's in this general direction. You don't like it, you're free to walk home."

"Don't be an asshole," Henry snapped.

"Listen, you." Digger jabbed a finger. "If you think I'm being an asshole now, just wait until we—" Shadows rushed from behind a tree. "Oh shit!" he yelped, fumbling for the revolver.

A powerful flashlight clicked on, blinding them. "All of you! Don't move or we'll blow your goddamned heads off!"

Janelle covered her eyes, but moments later the beam fell to her feet. Two men stood in the pool of light, one tall and burly with a thick red beard and shiny bald head, the other bent with age, his skin like age-spotted rice paper. In addition to the flashlight, the older man carried an automatic pistol.

The bearded man brandished a camo-finish AR-15 with a flashlight attachment. "Put the gun down, son. We're police officers."

Digger hesitated, then dropped the pistol into the grass and raised his arms over his head. Neither of the men wore uniforms or carried badges. They were dressed like the rest of the Kolchaks, in drab, faded camo and mismatched thrift store castoffs. Janelle considered taking off into the darkness until the bearded man swung the barrel in her direction. "Hold steady there, missy," he ordered. "No running. Everyone stay calm and don't do anything sudden. All right?"

"I killed you," Digger muttered.

The cop chuckled. "You can't kill me, son. Now, where's my money?"

Digger frowned. He dug into his coat pocket and handed over the envelope.

"Okay," the cop said. "We're all gonna walk nice and easy back the way you came. You try to run, and I'll shoot you in the legs."

"If you're the police, why are you taking us back to the criminals?" Janelle asked, already knowing the answer. "I was kidnapped and put in a cage. Why don't you help us escape?"

"I *am* here to help you, sweetheart." The cop grinned. His teeth were stained red. "You'll all be busy thanking me once you get to Paradise."

TWENTY-THREE

DIGGER MADE SMALL CRYING noises as he limped along at gunpoint.

"The fuck is wrong with you?" the cop asked. "Be a man."

"I stepped on a fuckin' nail! It fuckin' hurts, okay?" Digger snarled.

The elderly Kolchak snorted. "Soft."

The cop motioned with the muzzle of the rifle. "Just keep walkin'. You can sit and sob in your cage."

Henry shook his head, embarrassed for his friend, but scared too. Janelle had her eyes on the ground as she walked, looking dejected. His legs trembled. They were all going to die, he felt it in his gut.

Digger glared at the man with the gun, full of false bravado. "Shoulda double-tapped you."

"But you didn't, boo hoo. Walk, boy. And keep the snivelin' to a minimum."

Digger stopped. "Listen. I have a proposition—"

The cop rushed up to him, jabbing the gun in his face. "I said, get moving!"

"No, listen. You take them. Let me go, and I'll bring back... I don't know, *three* more people for you. You need bodies, right? I can get them for you. It's not like I can go to the cops, right? I'll give you my license and my car key. The license has my dad's home address on it. I love him more than life itself and would never put him in danger. You can trust me on that. If you let me go, I'll bring you whatever you want. *Anything*. Cars, people, drugs. Guns—I got direct access to a shitload of guns." His voice was high, the words rushed, but underneath the fear was something else. Excitement. "I can bring them out here today. Take me a few hours."

The cop shook his head. "So, you'd throw your friends under the bus to survive?"

Digger grimaced, avoiding Henry's eyes. "Look. I'm a realist. You guys got your thing going out here, however messed up it is, and I respect that. What I'm saying is: I can be more valuable to you alive than dead."

Henry couldn't believe what he was hearing. "What the fuck?"

Digger shot him a dark look. "Shut up, Henry. You'd do the same if you were smart enough to think it up first. You're just pissed you can't copy me like you always do."

The words stung. Henry had once imagined himself in love with Digger, but over time, those feelings had diminished. Now he realized that it wasn't love he'd felt, but desperation. Without Digger, he was alone. Their *deep friendship* was a convenient fiction he'd constructed over the years. One-sided. This wasn't a new Digger he was seeing, but the one that had been there all along. A fake hero. An appealing bully. But more than all of that, Henry was ashamed of his fantasies. And sick to his stomach how he'd used them to hold himself back, to believe that this was all he had. That following this man-child around was all he deserved in life.

And what did he think was going to happen? That Digger would finally realize the depth of their connection, and they would fuck (chaste, vanilla, in the least aggressive and soft-core way), then live together forever? Portland partners? Buy a fixer-upper Craftsman and a vintage Subaru, eat Thai food on Hawthorne, and hold hands while watching movies at the Hollywood Theater?

It was all a miserable, pathetic lie.

In reality, Digger was a stunted, perpetually stoned adolescent, who fell in love with every woman who would give him the time of day. Fucking many of them, but never committing to anyone. He treated Henry like shit but was careful not to go too far. Henry was his "yes man", his minion, the loser little bro he couldn't shake, and didn't really want to. All Henry wanted was to not be alone. Some days, it seemed like the inertia of their relationship could keep them together forever, bickering senior citizens; Digger with his eyes on a passing woman's ass, Henry with his eyes on Digger, the man he could never have.

Now though, considering all that had happened, the fantasy seemed horrible, unbearable, but if it brought Digger down to his level, well...

Light-headed and breathless, Henry snickered.

"What are you laughin' about?" Digger demanded.

"You. It's nice to finally see you for what you are."

"Shut up. *Fag*. I can't believe I ever was your friend. You don't deserve friends. Oh, that's right, I forgot—*you don't have any.*"

"Ladies!" the cop said. "Enough squabbling. Let's get a move on!"

Back at the tin shed, the campfires had been re-lit, and manic, torch-bearing Kolchaks caromed among the ruined cars like greasy pinballs. The only empty cage (the one they had escaped from) had a hole in its side, so the cop secured their wrists and ankles with zip ties and made them sit in the dirt. A mad-eyed Kolchak woman ran shrieking from the darkness to slash at Janelle with a kitchen knife, and she scuttled backward as best she could while restrained. The cop swore, cracking the woman in the face with the muzzle of his rifle until she ran off spitting blood and teeth. Henry took it in like it was a movie, numb, unable to care either way. Digger lay curled up on his side in the dirt, his eyes screwed shut.

Bruce Banner and Bailey Jean rounded the cages. Bruce was pulling a child-sized red wagon with a stiff-legged, gore-streaked fawn lying in it. The cop perked up. "Wow. Successful hunt, wee man?"

Bruce Banner licked his lips, putting his hand on the butt of the pistol tucked into his waistband. "Fresh roadkill, smart ass. Coo Coo brought it in, and Bailey Jean agrees with me we should throw it in the Cavity."

The cop shouldered his rifle. "Good thinking. Let's throw all these fucks in along with it. What we waitin' for?"

"The sun." Bailey Jean rubbed her temple. The dark hollows under her dull brown eyes spoke of cheap amphetamines and sleepless nights. "We'll begin the feast at dawn. Uchoa spoke of seeing it in her vision."

"They going in cooked or uncooked?" The cop picked at his teeth with a grubby yellow thumbnail, then spat into the grass. "If it's a BBQ I can start the prep."

"They'll meet the rising sun with a fiery blaze of their very own. The Cavity prefers them that way."

"Okey dokey smokey."

Digger sobbed into his arms. "Oh Jesus, no. What the hell, you guys? Really?"

Twenty-Four

However long Dorothea explores, she always finds herself back at the center of the Spiral, waiting patiently until the brooding entity notices her. It speaks the same words every time.

Ummmm, silver thing, why do you persist in haunting me?

With all the time in the world, she feels playful. A game, then. "I'm not haunting you. I *am* you. We're the same."

Then you hunger, as I do.

"Yes. But why are we so hungry all the time?"

We feed the whole. We eat and grow ever larger. There is no end to us, as there was no beginning. The hunger is the purpose, and in time, all will be us, and we will be all of it. There is no other way.

"How will this hunger ever be satisfied? Or can it be?"

It can. When we are all things. When we grow mouths numerous enough to devour the everything.

"But you only have the one. How will you devour everything with one mouth?"

Foolish thing. We are all mouths—if you could just see. Push yourself beyond the babble of silver ghosts, and witness how a thousand, thousandfold mouths gulp the rain. Soon, our hunger will become theirs, and these new mouths will swallow more than water from the sky... They will grow sufficient teeth to swallow all and everything, howling together to stun our prey... Then all are subsumed into the whole.

The way the entity communicates is frustrating. Like riddles from a sphinx. "But where are these mouths you speak of? I don't understand."

Understanding can be given. Sight can be bestowed. Come as close as you dare.

Dorothea has never ventured into the entity's space. She's always kept herself slightly apart, fearing what she might upset or find there. Throwing caution away, she inserts her awareness into the strange void of the center point. The entirety of the Spiral lights up around her, glowing, like the bodies of men and animals she'd seen through the eyes of the mouse. Each root shines like liquid fire, down to the tiniest hairs and fibers, and directly above her, the great, snapping Cavity blazes like the sun. Silver orbs dart around the edges, a confused mass of them, distracting from the perfection of the whole. Gauging the size of it all, she is struck dumb. The network extends for miles, underpinning the stunted forest, the scattered camps of the Kolchaks, and even the ranks of poisoned warehouses and empty lots girding the dead-end asphalt roads.

Do you not see them, silver thing? We thought you were keener than the ones that came before.

Slowly, the patterns in the Spiral become clearer: the broad pathways upon which she travels, the smaller roots reaching the surface, and the delicate fibers, the root hairs drinking in rain and nutrients that sustain the whole. Straining her perception, Dorothea finally sees what the entity is referring to. At regular intervals along the pathways, there are fist-sized nodes, harder to see at first due to their color, not yet glowing, but painted in shades of gray and black a few degrees lighter than the surrounding earth. She leaves the center, moving to the closest node. It takes a moment to recognize what she's seeing, but once she does, it all makes a kind of perverse sense. Naturally, something more is needed to sustain the whole, to feed the hunger, a *second* evolution, like meat-eating, to push the collective beyond current limitations. The Spiral is creating new spirals of its own.

A self-regenerating system.

"Will these grow larger?" she asks.

With assistance.

"What kind of assistance?"

Each must hold a silver thing, with a voice of its own. You will go to them, tell them where they must go, and what we all must do.

Dorothea returns to the very center and turns in place, taking in the spectacle of it all. Neither humans nor animals have the slightest idea of what lies in wait beneath their feet.

She begins to count. "Oh, shit."

The thousand Cavities pulse, eager to open and cry out, like the insistent mouths of baby birds demanding they be fed.

TWENTY-FIVE

JANELLE SQUEAKED, JERKING AWAKE from a nightmare. It was lighter now, almost dawn. A teen boy with a ragged ginger mullet was sitting in the dirt beside her. The heady musk he exuded was almost too much to bear.

"Here," he said, offering a battered plastic water bottle half-filled with clear liquid. "Drink this. It will make things a lot easier."

Thirsty and disoriented, she opened her mouth. Fire coursed down her gullet, and gagging, she retched into the grass. "Not...water..."

"It ain't that bad," the boy said, taking a sip himself. "You *wanna* be drunk when they light you up. Feelin' no pain."

Janelle spat, a thick rope of saliva hanging from her burning lips. "Fuck off."

Ordered about by the bearded cop, bleary-eyed Kolchaks lugged tires into the circle of stripped cars as Bailey Jean and another

135

woman hurried from cage to cage, whispering in each other's ears and writing in a blue spiral notebook. Digger hadn't moved from his fetal position, and Henry was sleeping, head slumped over his bound hands and feet. Feral dogs lurked in the early morning fog, hungry, wet-fur ghosts slinking around the edges of the camp. Janelle's butt was numb, pins and needles all up and down her legs.

"Hey," she whispered, nudging Henry with her toe. "You awake?"

His eyes flickered open. "Yeah."

She raised her zip-tied wrists. "You know how to get out of these? Anybody ever showed you?"

He shook his head no.

"It's easy. Take the hanging end in your teeth and pull it tight as you can. After you stand up, put your arms over your head then bring them down fast and hard, elbows going back and apart. They'll snap in two, it works."

He shrugged. "Even if we get out, they'll catch us. Or shoot us. We're gonna fucking die here."

"Jesus, Henry. Don't give up. That's what they want. We can always—"

In the thinning gray of the overcast morning, a cry went up. Four actual Portland Police officers wearing riot gear—helmets and body armor—and aiming AR-15s, had emerged from the trees. They fanned out in a semi-circle, while the slack-jawed Kolchaks stopped whatever they were doing to gawk.

"Bailey Jean!" The lead cop, a pear-shaped black man, pointed his rifle. "Where are you? What the fuck is going on around here? Where's Viktor?"

Pen and notebook in hand, Bailey Jean walked out to meet them. She waved, appearing unperturbed. "Hey, Ronnie."

The cop looked pissed. "Hey, what? Where the fuck is Viktor, you fat bitch? There was no drop yesterday. Making us come out here to this fuckin' dump is not what anybody wants. I'll round all you shitbirds up and then you can go sit in county. So don't say fucking 'Hey Ronnie' to me like it's nothing."

The bearded cop—*Viktor?*—jogged out of the fog waving an envelope. "Ron! Hey, sorry man. I have your money right here. Things got a bit out of hand earlier today, but we're good. I'm totally sorry, dude."

The cops lowered their weapons. Hitting a vape he'd taken from a pocket in his tactical vest, one cop exhaled a cloud of blue smoke as two others peered inside the cages, laughing at some inside joke.

Ronnie snatched the envelope from Viktor and thumbed through the stack of bills inside. "Looks like you're getting ready to have a little fun." He wrinkled his nose. "You know this shit out here is all NHI to me, Vik. I don't give a royal rat's ass what you do, as long as the donations keep coming in. But the envelope *gotta* be at the fucking drop, and I cannot. Stress. This. Enough—on *muthafucking* time! Comprende?"

"It won't happen again, I swear." Viktor scratched his beard. "And, well, I feel terrible making you guys trek out here. Listen, I got good beer on ice and an uncracked bottle of Johnnie Walker Blue in my trailer. Come have a drink with me before you go."

Ronnie looked inquisitively at the other cops and then shrugged. "Eh. Why not? Long walk back, and we're off the clock."

"Seriously?" Henry hissed.

The people in the cages shouted and cursed at the cops, hammering against the bars. The crazy woman wailed and gibbered.

Digger wriggled up onto his backside, apparently awake now, and tried to flex his arms. "Portland pigs. What did you expect? A.C.A.B."

With the group of men out of sight and the cages quieted, Bailey Jean rounded up the crew that was moving tires. "The feast begins at full light," she said to all assembled. "At the top of every hour, we feed two more penitents into the Cavity."

A new round of banging and outrage rose from the cages. Digger whimpered, pressing at the dried blood on his sneaker with bound hands. Janelle ignored it all, she'd found an Amstel Light bottle cap in the dirt by her feet and was busy pushing it into the locking mechanism of the zip tie that bound her ankles.

"Quiet!" Bailey Jean shouted. "You're all bound for Paradise! The crying is done! Soon it will be the time for endless celebration! Are you with me? We are all food, a banquet for God!" The

Kolchaks responded, circling her, taking up her words in a chant. "Food. For. Paradise. Food. For. Paradise."

Henry groaned. "Fuck. They're gonna burn us alive. Fuck!"

Janelle nudged him again. "Hold tight. Don't give up. I have an idea."

TWENTY-SIX

HENRY'S HUSBAND LOOKED A lot like Digger, but shorter, and the house was a mash-up of the house he'd grown up in and his friend Ciara's parents' home in Lake Oswego. He and the hubby were having breakfast in their kitschy cool kitchen, omelets and fresh squeezed orange juice, patty sausage with maple syrup, buttery biscuits. Hubby looked up, grinning over his half-finished plate. "How's it all taste, babe? I think I'm getting *a lot* better at cooking. Thanks to you, of course."

"I—uh, duts, ub, lig..." Henry stammered, his lips flapping, the words coming out in a string of gibberish. He was fucking up, like usual, and he knew it. "Glah—guh—good..."

"Thanks, baby," Hubby replied. "Maybe I'll try and whip up a dinner next."

Henry knew it was all a dream because, in it, he was happy. He jerked awake on the cold, hard ground, a halo of broken glass around his head. Kolchaks screaming. Chilly dew coated his hair and coat. He was going to die, or maybe he was dead already. Janelle kept nudging him with her toe.

"Henry, stop passing out," she whispered. "You need to stay awake if we're going to get out of this."

"I wanna sleep," he said. "Sleep for-fucking-ever."

"Oh, God. Shut up, quit cryin'," Digger said. "Such a little bitch."

"You shut up, pussy. Where's your .38? The big man with his big gun. You're the one crying."

Janelle sighed. "You guys, this is not helping at all."

Weak sunlight had finally crested the trees, warming him a bit. The Kolchaks congregated around the cages passing a jug and chattering like they were having a day out at the county fair. Janelle's eager-beaver-cum-heroic act was an annoyance. She said she had an "idea", like they all were all supposed to wait breathlessly for her to save them with her brilliant plan.

The hard-eyed woman in charge, Bailey-something-or-other had donned a spray-painted bike helmet and a loose blue robe or kaftan printed with stylized cranes. She pointed at Digger. "That one there can go first, and please pull the horrible screamer out of her cage. Let's get her gone, I'm sick of hearing it."

Two burly Kolchaks yanked Digger to his feet.

"No, what are you doing?" Henry tried to roll over, heart hammering against his ribs. It was *real*, and it was happening now, these freaks were going to kill them—starting with Digger. "Take someone else first. *Take someone else!*"

Digger dug in his heels, face a pale, panicked mask as they dragged him away. "Henry, help!" he begged. Tears welled at the corners of his eyes. "Don't let them fucking burn me, please, anyone, Henry, help! *Help!*"

TWENTY-SEVEN

TIME MEANS LITTLE IN the Spiral. Dorothea senses day and night through changes in pressure and the warmth or coolness of the ground around her, but minutes, hours, even days pass without notice. Most of the time, she finds herself *drifting*, either reliving her past or simply listening to the sounds of the living Earth. She feels her identity slipping away, her personhood diluted in the vast network of roots and fibers. The hunger of the entity has become her own and she dreams of what it might take to grow large enough to devour a city. The Kolchaks feed flesh into the Spiral, and now that is all it desires. The entity whispers orders, telling Dorothea what it expects her to do. A part of her wants to resist, to preserve what little autonomy she has left, but the pull of the Spiral is too great. She's terrified of losing herself completely but at the same time deeply flattered that the entity recognizes her value.

Guide each of the silver things to its place. They are aimless without you. Speak with them as you know how. Soon they will hunger as we hunger. Each one to its home, to wait, to wait...

This is no small task. Many of the sacrifices that exist within the Spiral are unstable, if not insane. Beaten, immolated, dismembered—they now find themselves trapped in a confusing afterlife they never imagined. This isn't the heaven their religions promised. Most of the victims are drug addicts, people with mental difficulties. People discarded by society. They were easy targets for the Kolchaks. Dorothea lies to them, saying whatever she thinks they need to hear, cajoling them into place with promises of Hell, Paradise, or rebirth. The true believers, such as the old man from the night they'd both been murdered, are the easiest to manipulate. He still thinks he's headed to Paradise, believing this to be a waiting room, purgatory, and happily moves to a Cavity when instructed to do so. Once the last silver thing is in place, she casts her awareness across the Spiral. Over a third of the fledgling Cavities are now occupied by a glimmering presence. It shows how many the Kolchaks had murdered, feral beasts feeding the very monster that would soon devour it.

Dorothea goes to her Cavity and settles in. It cups her, and she is like a fist in the ground, or a Venus flytrap, ready for flesh and bone, skin, fur, and feathers. The entity continues to broadcast its hunger, like a drumbeat, the message rippling through the Spiral, and each Cavity responds in turn, quivers with anticipation.

Dorothea feels the phantom pangs of hunger. She longs to stretch her consciousness, longs for the gush of hot blood into the earth, the filling and satiation. But, in addition to the primitive urges of the entity, she also longs for something more. Something larger. Something personal.

Revenge.

Twenty-Eight

JANELLE LEANED FORWARD ON her bound hands, grateful she hadn't been chosen as one of the first victims. Digger and the woman in the cage would die, it was already too late for them, but she would make her move, escaping while the Kolchaks were busy with murder. A cold calculation, but one born of necessity, and if it failed, well then, she would be dead, too. Henry lay on his side, hyperventilating, clearly panic-stricken for his friend. Janelle had a feeling their squabbling was all for show. Henry had made it to his feet only to be brutally knocked down again. He writhed in the trash and broken glass at the foot of the cage, white-faced, his bound hands bright pink.

"There's nothing you can do for him," she whispered. "Focus. You and I can still get out of this."

"Shit," he whimpered between gritted teeth. "He's only here because of me. It's like I killed him."

"Henry. This is not your fault. These people are homicidal maniacs. They can't be reasoned with. Listen to what I'm saying, and both of us will make it out of here."

Henry put his hands over his face, and Janelle saw that his fingernails were bitten to the quick. "How?"

"I told you the way to break your zip ties. Do you remember?"

He sniffled. "Over my head, then down and back."

"Exactly. And when they're busy with whatever they're going to do, we break out. Don't look. Don't think. Run for it. They catch us, we find weapons and fight. Anything. We go down swinging if it comes to that. It's a lot better than getting burned alive."

Henry stared at her for a full ten seconds before speaking. "I want to save Digger."

"That is not possible." The words came out slowly, like she was lecturing a child. "Don't be stupid. Henry, listen to me. The most you'll do is die alongside him."

"So, I just let my friend be murdered?"

"Do you want to live?"

Another long pause. "Of course I do."

"Then live for him. Set up a memorial. Make a foundation. I don't know. Get revenge. Tell the newspapers. These freaks can't have bought *all* the cops. But to do any of that, we *need* to get out of here alive."

Henry rolled onto his back, balling his swollen hands into fists, and stared at the line of wispy white clouds floating across the morning sky. "These will snap off if I do what you said?"

"Yes. I'll tell you when I think it's best to go, and we'll run for it while they're occupied."

"Then what?"

"Keep running until we find help. Fight if we must."

"Okay."

"Okay?"

"I'm not a good fighter."

"But you're a good runner, I bet. Most not good fighters are."

"Hmm. Yeah. Guess so."

A metallic rhythm started up, interrupting them. The drumming echoed across the shallow valley, alien and mechanical, as dogs howled in the distance and the crows wheeled overhead.

Henry raised his head. "What *is* that?"

"They're banging on the cars, I think."

As if summoned by the noise, the remaining Kolchaks rose and shambled in the direction of the Cavity, leaving only two behind to guard the cages. The mutilated teen boy, who now sported a long kitchen knife stuck in his belt, and Bruce Banner.

"I got a bottle of Ten High hidden in the shed," Bruce said. "Be right back."

The teen boy smacked his lips, grinning. "Mmm, Ten High. What's that? Eight bucks a fifth? Drinkin' the good stuff these days eh?" He snickered.

"You get none then," Bruce said over his shoulder.

"Hey! I'm just kiddin' around! Jokes!" The boy squinted at the ground. "Ugh, I need a fuckin' butt." He then zig-zagged down the line of cages looking for something to smoke. Once he'd turned a corner out of sight, Janelle leaped to her feet.

Having already broken the zip tie on her ankles with the bottle cap, she raised her hands over her head and brought them down fast, freeing her wrists. Henry kicked his feet until the ankle tie was broken, but it took three tries to free his wrists, leaving deep, red welts on the pale, doughy flesh.

Janelle snatched up a garden rake left leaning against one of the plastic chairs. "Let's go. If you see anything you can use as a weapon, grab it."

Henry grimaced, then took off running in the direction of the Cavity, the Kolchaks—and Digger. "I'm sorry!" he shouted.

Janelle banged the butt of the rake on the ground in frustration. "Oh, come on! Henry, don't do this!"

TWENTY–NINE

DROWSY FROM SPAGHETTI LUNCH, Henry sensed the sucker punch moments before it connected with his temple. He swore, tumbling into the bushes next to the steps of the little gym, losing his backpack in the process.

Lying in the dirt, he had no desire to move, no desire to think or care, but Tim Winnaker kicked his sneaker, a sneering grin stretched across his blotchy bulldog features. "You like that, faggot? You and that big mouth of yours get turned on when an alpha touches you? Come on, get up and fight, faggot."

A small crowd had gathered, kids in their wrinkled gym clothes, some holding hydro flasks, each of them eager to witness a beating. A tall, lanky boy with long auburn hair stepped from the jostling students.

"Jesus, Tim, fuckin' leave him alone." Digger rolled his eyes. "You know he's not gonna fight you."

"Shut up, hippy, or you're next." The bell rang, and Winnaker glanced at his wristwatch. "Shit." He pointed at Henry. "I gotta go, but keep talking out your ass and I'll break those lardy fucking hams you call legs, understand?"

Henry frowned, rubbing the red mark on his forehead. "I *got* it."

"You better. I'm late to meet my fucking stupid guidance counselor." Tim shouldered his backpack and hurried off.

The disappointed crowd drifted away as Digger helped Henry to his feet. "You *could* fight him, you know. He's not that tough. Even if you lost, he'd probably lose interest and move on to somebody else."

Red-faced, Henry snatched his backpack from the bush. Digger was a year younger than him but seemed so...so...*confident*. How did he do it? How did any of them do it? Adolescence was like a stupid mystery he'd never been able to solve.

This wasn't the first time Digger had stepped up to defend him. Their moms were friends— part of the same gardening group—and they'd hung around, on and off, since middle school. Digger was the cool and popular one, always invited to girls' parties, or out to drink under the bleachers with the football team. He wasn't even an athlete. To Henry, this all seemed totally unfair. Digger made it seem so easy.

"I have an idea," he said. "Why don't you fight him for me?"

Digger shook his head. "And you wonder why girls think you're a weak pussy. Even that weird, fat fuck Alejandro fights back."

"Look. Just leave me alone, okay?"

"No, I'm not gonna, dumbass. Lunch is almost over, let's ditch fifth period and go smoke. Might make your head feel better."

Henry sighed. One rude, annoying friend? Or no friends at all? Two more long years until he graduated. He quickly did the math. "Fine. You better get me super high, though."

Digger scoffed, pushing his hair from his eyes. "When have I not?"

Their favorite place to smoke when cutting class was a pair of empty lots a few blocks from the school. All that was left of the house that once stood there were a few broken pieces of the foundation, and a falling down chain-link fence. Gargantuan fir trees dominated one end of the property, while weeds and bushes had claimed the remainder. People would camp there from time to time but presently it was clear of tents. Peaceful. Fat bumblebees flew in lazy arcs from flower to flower, dusted with an embarrassment of pollen.

Digger led Henry to their regular spot and sat down cross-legged on a bed of pine needles. He pulled a lighter and packed bowl from his fanny pack and lit up, holding the smoke, with eyes closed, before exhaling it in a spinning gray cloud. Leaning back, he handed the bowl to Henry.

Henry took a hit, and blew it out, trying not to cough. He glanced covertly at Digger's bare, fuzzy legs until his friend opened his eyes. "Gimme." He reached for the bowl.

Henry handed it over. He already felt too high, anxious and wired. Digger only smoked the best sativa.

Digger took another big hit off the bowl. He exhaled and then shook his head. "Damn. Good shit."

"Yeah." Henry chuckled.

"Did you hear Daniel Kikorsky came out as gay?" Digger sat up straight, staring right at him.

"No," Henry lied. "Why would he do that?"

Kikorsky was even lower on the social totem pole than he was, a bespeckled, rail-thin, autistic mess of a kid. If the *was* gay, good for him, but Henry had no desire to associate himself with someone so unpopular.

"Well," Digger said. "'Cause he's gay. Why would anyone hide that? We're out of the stone age."

"Maybe it's nobody's business." The world began to fuzz up inside Henry's head, but he blinked it away. "Why? You don't care?"

Digger shrugged. "Guys with guys, girls with girls—what's the problem? Let everybody feel the way they want."

Henry rolled his eyes. "Last summer you said you hated fags."

"That was last summer. People change, you know. Grow up. And Melanie said she thinks it's cool when guys are bi. It's being open-minded."

Melanie Rao, captain of the girl's volleyball team, was Digger's latest crush. "Wow. She said that? Would you ever try being bi?"

"I dunno. Maybe. Who knows? Depends on the person, and the situation. I want to try lots of things." The lighter flared as Digger hit the bowl again. He exhaled and handed it over. "It's almost cashed. Finish it."

Henry took the bowl, but he didn't smoke. A small, glowing kernel of hope had been ignited in his heart. He saw his friend in a new light, one that he never thought he'd see, and felt like he was about to hyperventilate.

Digger snorted, his eyes reduced to slits. "What are you waiting for, Henry? Toke up."

Henry hit the pipe.

THIRTY

HENRY DODGED PAST KOLCHAKS too surprised, too stupid, or too drugged out to stop him. Digger had been forced to his knees in front of the ditch that held the cryptid. A dripping tire hung from his neck.

Henry grabbed the tire and flung it at the closest Kolchak, the pungent gas fumes prickling in his throat. "Get up, get up!" He pulled on Digger's arms. The element of surprise was lost, and a mob of armed Kolchaks, including the bald cop, were shouting, and running his way.

Digger wobbled; half-lidded eyes bright pink from the gasoline bath. "Wha? Fuck, Henry, I think they're killing me."

A Kolchak grabbed Henry in a bear hug, but he managed to stomp the man's ankle and squirm out, stumbling over the uneven ground. After a delayed reaction, Digger was on his feet, throwing drunken haymakers to little effect. A Kolchak ducked under his fists, but then tripped over her own feet, sprawling at the crumbling edges of the ditch. The creature snapped shut with a *crack* like a triggered bear trap and dozens of insectile legs sprouted from the ground around it, clawing at the woman. Henry kicked her square in the face, and she fell backward, screaming as the horrible chitinous legs latched onto her clothing. Another Kolchak tried to tackle Henry but tripped over the gasoline-soaked tire. Then Janelle, who he'd already figured long gone, charged up swinging the rusty rake.

"Get him up and run," she gasped. "I'll try and hold them off!"

Henry took hold of Digger's elbow. "You have to come too. Don't sacrifice yourself!"

Janelle made a bewildered face. The Kolchaks lurked a few yards away, just out of rake range. One lunged, and she swung at the woman's head. "Of course, I'm coming! Go!"

THIRTY-ONE

DOROTHEA JOINS THE CHORUS of shrieks, then strikes the warm glow directly above.

The small Cavity she controls opens, and the circular fringe of writhing fingers directs the unsuspecting Kolchak into her spongy gullet. Snapping shut on a pair of legs, she severs them in half. Salty blood flows in rich rivulets, a wash of hot gore. The cultist howls, writhing in agony, but Dorothea registers their cries as little more than a distant buzz. Like a heron with a wriggling fish in its beak, she opens and gulps once more. The halved remnant of the shining body falls, disappearing below the ground. A thick, caustic fluid stills the prey's final, feeble kicks. Dorothea is pleased with how fast the Kolchak dissolves, the savage efficiency of it all, and how little it satiates her hunger.

More.

Within two minutes, she is poised to strike again, ready to feast anew.

A pair of chattering figures pause above her, and she expands the Cavity's circumference, accordion-like, to take them both. The voices of the living are a babble, little more than the soughing of the wind, but one of these voices strikes a nerve. It's...something she once knew, a hazy memory of another world, another life, something close, and dear, and important...

"Henry, it's too late. I'm sorry, we must go."

Janelle?

The ground rumbles, tiny shockwaves passing through the Spiral as it feasts, gorging on torn flesh and cracked bone. Puzzled into inaction by the familiar voice, Dorothea allows the targets to pass on. A dream flits across what is left of her: a sister, dark-eyed, curling, and warm under the covers, they lie together, safe, loved. But just as quick as it comes the dream fades to nothingness. In its place is hunger. Need. Dorothea returns to the feast; returns to the place she is now meant to be.

And all around, a hundred Cavities bloom, violently welcoming dozens of new shining things into the realm of their collective will. Today, carnage reigns supreme, but even when it is finished, the hunger of the Spiral remains far from satiated.

THIRTY-TWO

JANELLE SWIPED THE RAKE, forcing the knot of Kolchaks back. "Stay behind me," she told Henry and Digger. "And move!"

Red-faced, Bailey Jean bulled her way through the crowd. "Viktor! Get over here and shoot this bitch!" She smacked a Kolchak on the back of his head. "What are you waiting for? Rush her! She won't be able to stop you all!"

"Get back!" Janelle lashed out. Still wary, the Kolchaks circled to either side, searching for an opening.

"Viktor!" Bailey Jean shrieked.

Henry supported Digger as they stumbled toward the cages. "I know you're hurt," he was telling his friend, "But it's important we move fast."

Wild-eyed, Digger shrugged him off. "No. F-fuck you. I'm going this way; you go that way. You're—you're bad luck, dude. I could fight *all* these assholes if I wanted to. But I'm not saving a weak shit like you. Not anymore."

Shamed into action by Bailey Jean, three Kolchaks ran at Janelle. One was armed with a nail-studded two-by-four, which he swung at her head. Janelle parried the two-by-four with the rake, and its wooden handle splintered, the head skittering behind the flattened tire of a ruined Chevy Blazer. Janelle turned and ran, dropping the useless length of wood. Frantically looking around, she spied a fist-sized stone on the ground. Janelle flung the stone and hit the Kolchak in the upper thigh, surprising herself. He went down yowling. Seeing him hit by the rock, his friends either slowed their attack or scattered.

After catching up with Henry, she saw Digger had veered off and was now headed in a different direction. A gun cracked, and a small plume of dust rose in the grass a few feet away. The Kolchaks were still coming.

"Henry, what's going on? Run!"

"I-I—" He gesticulated helplessly. "He won't listen to me. I think he hit his head. He's not in his right mind."

"Digger!" Janelle called out. "Come with us!"

Without stopping, or turning around, Digger raised a middle finger.

Henry flapped his arms. "You see?"

Janelle flinched as another shot rang out, a high-pitched plink, probably someone with a varmint rifle. "You saved him once, but he's an adult and can make his own decisions." She couldn't even believe she was even having this conversation. "I'm going *right now* Henry, come with me."

"You don't understand—*aaahh*!" Henry recoiled, grimacing like he'd been stung.

The high-pitched tone stabbed Janelle's eardrums, and she covered her ears. From what she could see the noise affected everyone, with no clear source. The Kolchaks were crying out, on their knees from the pain, or running around madly.

Digger stumbled, covering his ears. A sinkhole opened beneath his feet, and he dropped inside. Panting, confused, he tried to climb out, but the hole snapped shut around his waist. He beat at the grass, screaming in agony like he was being assaulted. Janelle watched, paralyzed, trying to understand what was happening to him. Moments later, he slumped over and lay still.

"Digger!" Henry ran toward his friend.

Janelle followed. It didn't look good. Digger was twitching, unresponsive, with a large quantity of blood soaking through his jacket. His eyes rolled. "Buh... Bru... He..." Blood dribbled over his pale lips.

Before Henry had gone more than a few feet, the sinkhole released its hold, widening, and Digger sank inside. The earth then snapped shut over him, as if the hole had never existed in the first place. Henry fell to his knees where his friend had disappeared and began digging with his hands. "Hold on! Hold on!"

The noise trailed off. Janelle wobbled, feeling light she might pass out.

Viktor appeared, waving his rifle. "All right, cupcakes, back we go again. Don't make me shoot you. The Cavity prefers its meat cooked alive."

"Don't you see what's happening?" Janelle asked.

A sinkhole opened beneath Viktor's feet, and he slipped inside with a surprised grunt. "What the fuck?"

The hole snapped shut like an alligator's jaw, and Viktor cried out, face instantly blanched white, eyes bulging. He dropped the AR-15 to paw at the dirt and grass around him.

"Whaaa..." He reached out a trembling hand to Janelle as blood trickled from under his vest. It appeared he'd been crushed or maybe even bitten in half. More dark blood foamed over his twitching lips. Viktor's eyes glazed over, and the hole opened once more to suck down what remained of him.

Paralyzed by fear, Janelle watched the carnage unfold. Kolchaks were screaming and dying, running for their lives as dozens of strange holes appeared, only to snap shut with violent force, severing limbs and in some cases, even swallowing the victims whole.

The Earth was eating people alive.

"Help. Help me." A woman lying on her back in a patch of tall weeds beckoned to her.

Drawing closer, Janelle saw it was the woman from the van, the woman who had assaulted her. She was bitten half, nothing but bloody, trailing intestines below the cracked leather belt, her long, greasy dreads spread out in the dirt like a halo of snakes. Face drained of all color; she wasn't long for this world. Janelle kneeled, taking the woman's hand.

"Where—where's Uchoa?" the woman asked, black blood welling over her lips.

"I don't know," Janelle said. "Rest now."

Where there should have been hate and revulsion, all that was left was sadness, and a deep sense of pity. No matter what terrible things this woman had done, to end up like this was a terrible tragedy. Huge flies were already swarming, landing to lap at the warm, sticky pool of blood and feces.

Janelle dropped the dead woman's hand and ran back to Henry.

"Digger!" He was still pawing at the dirt, to little effect. "Digger, can you hear me?"

Janelle pulled him to his feet. "Henry, come on. It's too late. I'm sorry, let's go while we can."

The ground trembled, and she prepared to jump away if a hole opened, but the movement beneath her feet subsided. Severed limbs littered the field, along with the dead and dying. The few Kolchaks who had avoided being eaten had already fled. Whatever this was—and Janelle had a sinking suspicion it had something to do with the creature in the ditch—appeared to have finally ended.

Tears streamed down Henry's face, and he sniffled back a nose full of snot. "I—uh, I—uh, uh. I don't—I don't know how this happened. Do you think maybe he's still alive down there?"

Janelle shook her head. "I-I don't know. But I doubt he survived that. No one else that was caught did. Horrible." She took his hand, guiding him. "I'm sorry about Digger, Henry. You did the best you could. Now, let's go."

Henry stumbled along, rubbing his dirty, tear-streaked cheek. "Okay. Okay. I'm coming. I did my best. I tried. Okay. Okay."

THIRTY-THREE

HENRY CHUGGED THE CAN of Rainier, a cold six-pack sitting in his lap. Tossing the empty into the back seat of the Kia, he popped a second. It was stuffy in the car, but he kept the windows shut. His ears were sensitive from the...*attack*—he didn't know what else to call it—Digger's spare key still clutched in his sweaty palm. Massacre. That sounded better. It was a massacre. And Jack—Digger's dad—was all he could think about. What could he possibly tell Jack that wouldn't sound batshit crazy? Your son was eaten by the earth? By a monster? This had all turned into such a surreal mess.

"You should have one, too," he told Janelle. She was sitting in the passenger seat, looking out the window, hands folded in her lap, back straight and tight, like a spring ready to pop. Upon reaching the Kia they'd sat in shocked silence for twenty minutes before Henry had driven them to a convenience store and bought booze.

Janelle took the can but didn't open it.

"Will you take me to 33rd and Marine?" she asked. "Errol, the guy who kidnapped me, his RV is parked there. I want to talk to him as soon as possible."

Henry was wet and dirty. Exhausted, but awake. Wired. "Why? You gonna fuck him up?" He was only half kidding.

Janelle stared straight ahead. "Yes. He's got my phone. And probably my car, too. My mother's ashes are in the trunk."

"Oh, I'm sorry." Henry's face cycled through a range of conflicting emotions. "Condolences on your...your mom. You deserve to get those back, at least. What an asshole that guy is."

"I care more about the car and phone than the ashes. My mom... isn't worth my time anymore. And you're right, I want revenge, too. Will you take me?"

Henry put the Sportage into gear, happy to have something to do, some goal, anything but having to face grim reality. He needed time to think. Jack, and the world, could wait. "Fuck yeah. Car thieves are the lowest of the low. Let's find him and teach him a lesson. For Digger."

Janelle nodded, taking hold of the grab handle on the roof. "And Dorothea."

THIRTY-FOUR

"WHAT'S WRONG?" JANELLE ASKED.

Henry was sitting on his ratty couch, holding Digger's bong. He'd just exhaled a huge cloud of weed smoke when it hit him all over again. Digger was gone. There wasn't even a body to bury.

Dead. For real.

"I don't know—it's just—being back here, seeing all his, his stuff..." He sniffled, wiping his nose with the back of his hand. "It's hard, you know?"

"I know." Janelle put the half-finished plate of scrambled eggs she was holding on the dining room table. "Deep breaths. We've been through a lot." She walked to the couch and sat down next to him. "You should eat something. It'll help."

Henry shook the glass bong, watching the dirty water swirl around inside. "What are you going to do with your mom's remains once you get them back?"

Until an hour ago, Janelle had forgotten about the battered cardboard box she'd received from the funeral home. She hoped Errol hadn't realized there was anything in the trunk, or didn't care enough to mess with it. To tell the truth, she didn't care much now, either. With Dorothea gone too, it was hard to summon the energy for what now seemed like a pointless nicety.

"Regina wanted her ashes spread in the ocean, of course. At her favorite beach near St. Pete. But that seems like way too much effort now. How far is the ocean from here?"

"Oh. Hour and a half drive, maybe," Henry said.

Janelle stared at the box. "River's closer. Hey, it's water, and it flows down to the ocean, right?"

"I need a hot shower." Henry rose from the couch, and the baseball bat propped against it fell to the carpet with a thump. Janelle watched him leave, and moments later, heard running water.

Halfway to the homeless camp on 33rd, they'd run out of steam. Once they started talking in earnest about confronting Errol, they realized they were hungry, and thirsty, tired, and still in shock from all the carnage they'd witnessed. They would also need weapons. Errol was a violent criminal, and both doubted he would give up Janelle's possessions without, at minimum, being threatened with bodily harm.

Returning to her plate of cold eggs, she sat at the beat-up dining room table. The table was cluttered with random things: a pile of fishing magazines, a cracked motorcycle helmet, two empty (she assumed) pizza boxes, crusted silverware, and a plastic bin filled with miscellaneous Lego bricks. The table itself was old and scratched, like most of the furnishings in the house. Everything in the cramped living room was mismatched—thrift-store bargains mixed with what appeared to be castoffs from a college fraternity house. The whole place reeked like one, too.

Was *this* how gay men lived? If so, she'd been misinformed.

And that was another thing. She still couldn't figure out Henry and Digger's relationship. Were they cousins? Roommates? Boyfriends? Fuck buddies? It struck her as kind of a Peter Pan and Neverland situation, two men who decided they were going to remain boys forever. But now one of them was gone. Henry would have to grow up, to leave his Neverland. She could see why he was so upset.

Not that Janelle considered herself to be any better. She'd never even had a relationship, with any close friends counted on one hand. The mechanics of dating, and romance, and sex were abject mysteries to her. Sure, she'd seen the labels that people talked about online: *asexual, aromantic,* but she was still hesitant to apply them to herself, let alone announce them to the world. What if she changed her mind? What if she met someone, and suddenly all her feelings turned inside out? A 'bolt out the blue', like in trashy romance novels? True, there were times when she was quite lonely, but for the most part, being alone wasn't a bad life. And after seeing how Henry and Digger interacted, how they ended up, maybe she was content with things exactly the way they were.

Henry emerged from his bedroom in clean clothes, but his eyes were red and puffy. He held out a damp, rumpled towel. "Do you want to shower?"

Janell got up from the table, picking up her dirty cup and plate. "No, thanks. We should get going."

Henry retrieved the fallen baseball bat. "You still up for this?"

She had a feeling this was coming. "Yes. I have to. Why? Are you not?"

"No." Henry walked to the closet and opened it. "It's just... I'm lost. I don't know what to do anymore."

"Let's get my stuff back from Errol, and then I'll sit down with you, and we can sort all this out, okay?"

He nodded and sighed, bending over to rummage around in the closet. "There it is." He pulled out a golf putter. "How's your swing?"

Janelle took the putter. It was heavy and could do some damage. "Quit it. Let's go."

They parked Digger's Sportage in an empty lot behind a shuttered *Tool & Die* manufacturer. The For Sale sign on the building rippled in the wind, hanging sideways by a single nail. Henry had brought a duffel bag to hide the bat and putter, and they walked on the shoulder the rest of the way to the camp of broken-down RVs and stripped cars. Other than a stray cat licking itself on the center line, 33rd Street was deserted, all the businesses dark and closed for the night.

"That's Errol's RV, there," Janelle said, pointing to a spray-painted relic on the far end. She'd remembered it looking bad, but now it looked abandoned, with broken glass littering the road in front of it.

"*Candy Wagon*," Henry read. "Jesus H. Christ. This Errol guy must be messed up in the head."

"Oh, and look. That's my car hidden behind it," she said. "On top of a pile of trash, of course. Bastard. He better not have fucked up the tires."

Henry checked the street. It was still empty. No cars, nothing. Kneeling, he unzipped the duffel and removed the bat and putter. There was also a canister of pepper spray in the bag. He put the spray canister in his jacket pocket, then stood, brushing bits of gravel from his knees. Buoyed by chill winds, a new wall of gray clouds had marched in from the west, and a light, misting drizzle began to fall.

"All right." Janelle took the putter from him. "Time to see if he's home."

Seeing the RV up close confirmed her fears. The boards had been pried from the rear window and the top of the RV was blackened by soot. She pulled herself up on the broken window frame and peeked inside. More smoke damage. Every surface was covered in a layer of gritty white powder, probably from a fire extinguisher.

The headboard of the big bed was charred; with a burnt duvet and pillows scattered over the carpet.

Janelle dropped back down. "It's all burned out." She kicked an empty beer can into the street. "Shit. What do I do now? I need the fucking keys to my car. I want to get out of here, go back to fucking Tampa, and try to forget any of this ever happened."

"Is Tampa that much better than here?" Henry asked.

"No. But at least it's warm."

"Let's check the car, maybe the keys are in it. I wish I knew how to hotwire. We could steal it back."

Halfway around the back of the RV, Janelle stopped. "Wait. I forgot. I know somebody else here."

"You do?"

Janelle hurried off down the line of trash heaps and broken-down vehicles. Picking one seemingly at random, she knocked on the door. Moments later, the door opened, and a man stuck his head out. Almost immediately, Henry realized he'd seen that face before. It was the weird older man who'd propositioned him in the bathroom of the Compass and Sextant. With that greasy, died-black pompadour, there was no mistaking him. Janelle and the man just stared at one another, wide-eyed with surprise, both momentarily struck dumb.

"Who is it, Eddie?" A woman called from inside the RV.

"Just a pesky salesman, darlin'! Be right back." Errol stepped out, closing the door. He smiled big. "Janelle! Fancy seein' you here! You a Kolchak now?"

Janelle raised the putter, charging up a home-run swing. "Fucking piece of shit! Gimme my car keys! And my phone, before I break your lousy, kidnapping, head open!"

Errol flinched, raising his arms to protect himself. "Now, wait a minute! I can explain! I swear!"

Henry moved in on the other side, bat raised. "You heard her! Where's the key, asshole?!"

Errol moved like a snake, with a quick fake left, and ducked under the putter. Janelle swung and missed. He then took off running, long legs pumping furiously in his black Converse. A hundred yards down the road he left the asphalt, crashing through the weeds into a trash-strewn field littered with a dozen more stripped hulks of stolen cars and trailers. Janelle had almost caught up when Errol darted around a wheelless box truck sat atop cinder blocks. A door slammed. A long, windowless shed was hidden behind a truck. She tried the doorknob, but it was locked.

"Damn it!" Janelle hit the metal door with the putter, leaving a mark. "Errol, you piece of shit! Fucking murderer! Come out here and take your medicine! I want my goddamned keys and my phone!"

Janelle made a full circuit, flushing a startled baby rabbit from the weeds, to confirm what she'd suspected. The shed's front door was the only way in, or out. "Damn it."

Henry put a finger to his lips and motioned for her to follow him. Back on the road, out of earshot, he said: "Let's hide somewhere we can see the door. Errol's got to come out sooner or later."

Janelle shook her head. "Nah. I've got a better idea, come on."

Back at the line-up of RVs, she marched straight to the door of the one Errol was in and banged on the door with the putter. The woman who answered had her hair up in curlers, looking like she hadn't slept in days. Janelle vaguely remembered the smudged pink lipstick and liquor-bloated face from when she was here last. It was only the day before yesterday, but it seemed like a million years ago.

"Do I know you?" the woman asked. "What do you want?"

Janelle grabbed the woman by the front of her grimy housecoat and yanked her face first onto the asphalt.

The woman rolled onto her side and whimpered. There was blood on her lip. "Ow, shit. Why the hell'd you do that, lady? What I ever do to you?"

Janelle yanked on her collar. "Get up. We're going to see your friend, Eddie."

The woman rose, cupping her red, swelling chin. "That sweet-talking asshole. I should have known it was him. I really know how to pick 'em, don't I?"

When they reached the shed, Janelle grabbed the woman's arm, wrenching it up behind her back. "Now, call your boyfriend. If you don't, I'll break your arm."

"Ouch, shit. Okay. Take it easy," she sniffled. "Eddie! Eddie come out, before this bitch kills me. Eddie! Open the door, now!"

Janelle told Henry to wait out of sight, just around the corner of the shed. He nodded, and crept off, bat ready.

"Eddie, God damn it! What shit have you got me into this time?"

Metal scraped on metal, and the door creaked open just enough for Errol to peek through.

"Let Sonja go, Janelle," he said. "She's got no part in this. Let her go, and I'll give you what you want."

Janelle bent Sonja's arm even further, until she sobbed. "Give me the keys first, and I'll let her go. Do it!"

"Okay, I'm coming out," Errol said. "I got your keys right here in my pocket, right? Don't hurt my baby girl no more."

Rusted metal groaned as the door opened. Errol emerged, holding out an enamel keyring that said 'Florida', with a hula dancer underneath, the once-vibrant colors worn almost completely away.

"Here Janny," he said. "Take 'em, and go."

Henry popped out, bringing the bat down hard and fast on Errol's wrist. The keys flew into the weeds. "He's got a knife! Watch out!"

"Agh, dag!" Errol cried out in agony, grabbing his wrist as he fell to his knees. An open switchblade tumbled into the dirt. Janelle shoved Sonja hard, and the woman tumbled on top of him, then both collapsed together in a groaning heap.

Henry kicked the switchblade out of reach while Janelle hurried to retrieve her keys. Errol lay on the ground holding his wrist, tears leaking down his craggy face as Sonja tried to comfort him.

"I think you broke my GD arm!" he said. "Why the hell'd you have to do that, dude? I was already givin' her the damned things!"

"You were going to stab her," Henry said. "I saw you."

Errol flexed his wrist and grimaced. "It was for my protection, that's all. I'd never stab Janny. We go way back."

Janelle ran over and gave him a vicious kick in the back. He grunted, doubling over in pain. "Where's my phone?!" She kicked him again. "And what the *fuck* did you do to Dorothea?"

Sonja swatted half-heartedly at Janelle. "Don't you hurt Eddie no more!"

"Nothing! I swear! It's the truth!" he moaned. "She left me. I sold your phone right after I got it, I'm sorry!"

Henry walked to the shed door. He stuck his head inside and then retreated, frowning. "Hey. Some weird-sounding noises coming from in there." He looked at Errol with disgust. "What's that smell? This your meth shack? Are you cooking meth?"

"No!" Errol's face went beet red. "I got a TV on. Me n' Sonja like to watch *The Price is Right*!"

Janelle retrieved her putter. "I'll check it out. Make sure these two don't run off."

Henry loomed over them with his bat. "Gladly."

Inside, the shed was a single room lit by a dangling lightbulb. Miscellaneous trash, fast food wrappers, rat, and dog feces filled every corner. The stench was eye-watering, a mix of old cat piss, mold, and rotting fish. Janelle covered her nose. There was no TV, or furniture, just four tattered mattresses lined up on the filthy ground. Someone was lying on one of the mattresses.

"Hello?" Janelle said, her shoes crunching on the carpet of refuse. "Are you all right?"

The person wriggled, making muffled noises of distress. She stepped closer. "Hello?"

It was an androgynous woman, dressed in grubby jeans and a threadbare T-shirt. The woman was gagged, both her hands and feet tied with green duct tape. Her dark eyes rolled and blinked above the gag, filled with tears—a terrible sight in the waxy yellow gloom.

"Oh, shit," Janelle muttered. The woman began to squeal beneath the gag.

Lying among the trash piles were a few brand-new rolls of tape, and a pair of safety scissors. Using the scissors, Janelle freed the woman's feet and hands. She was barefoot, the soles black with engrained black filth. The woman immediately pulled the gag over her head and threw it away.

181

"Are you hurt?" she asked

The woman sat up. She was thin to the point of emaciation, covered in purple and yellow bruises "I don't like slow songs," she said.

"Do you need an ambulance? Can you walk?"

The woman blinked up at her, mouth hanging open a little. Her head had been unevenly shaved, tufted in some spots, shorn down to the scalp in others. "I don't like slow songs," she repeated.

"Uh huh. I got that. Did Errol, or maybe you know him as Eddie—tall guy, black hair, tie you up?"

The woman licked her fingers, unconcerned. "I don't...like slow songs."

Janelle backed away. "Oh-kay. Um, you're free to go. Errol won't try to stop you."

Continuing to lick her fingers, the woman said nothing.

Back outside, Errol was on his feet. Henry had him and Sonja backed against the shed. "What was in there?" he asked.

Janelle faked like he was about to hit Errol, and the man flinched, putting his arms over his face. "This sick fuck had a woman tied up in there. I let her go, but she doesn't seem in too good a state. Who knows what he did to her."

"No, you don't understand!" Errol said. "That bitch is stone cold crazy! I was doing everybody a service! Ask Sonja—right, honey?"

Sonja's head bobbled. "Nuttier than a Christmas fruitcake. Burned out the Candy Wagon. Lost all the pillow shams Memaw Dolores made me."

"You were going to give her to the Kolchaks," Janelle growled. "Like you did with me."

"Well, lemme just say about that, I'm truly sorry, Janelle." Errol put his hand over his heart. "I'm truly sorry, I was misguided, and I hope you can find it in your heart to forgive me."

"I don't like slow songs."

The woman was standing in the doorway of the shed, squinting from the gloom.

Janelle cleared her throat. "Hello there. I forgot to tell you my name. It's Janelle, what's yours?"

The woman appeared not to hear. She walked to the side of the shed, and squatted, digging in the weeds. What happened next was over so fast they didn't even have time to react.

The woman turned and lunged at Errol, his switchblade in her hand. She stabbed him underhand, sinking the blade into the meat of his thigh—fast, shallow jabs—one after another, five, or six, in all. Errol let out an agonized yowl, and the woman tossed the knife, running away into the bushes. He crumpled to the ground, crying pitifully as blood began to soak through his pants leg.

"What the fuck?!" Henry yelled.

"I told you!" Sonja took a bedazzled iPhone from her pocket and dialed 911. "We need an ambulance!" she screamed into the phone.

Janelle looked at Henry. He nodded, and then they both took off running onto 33rd Street, and the waiting cars.

They had to drive separately, but within the hour they were back safe at Henry's house. He ordered Domino's delivery on Digger's laptop, and they split a six-pack. After supper, Henry offered her a packed bong, but she politely declined.

Janelle yawned. "Jesus, what a day," she said, curled up on the couch, clutching a pillow to her chest. Henry had offered the couch for the night, and she'd accepted. "Have you decided what you're going to do about Digger's dad? Is he the only one that's going to be looking for him? What are you thinking about telling him? The truth?"

Henry blew out his cheeks. "I don't know. I can't go to the cops, 'cause they're in on it. I can't go to a newspaper, 'cause the story is too whacked out. Who's gonna believe me? They'll think that I killed him and hid the body. I'm screwed, as usual. Going to prison, most likely."

"You *could* say the Kolchaks killed him. I mean, technically, they did. And if they never find his remains—no body, no crime, right?"

That seemed to cheer Henry up a bit, or maybe it was the weed. "Yeah. Yeah! I have a few days, at least. What are you going to do now?"

"Go home, I guess. Start my life up again."

Henry fiddled with the bong, adjusting the stem. "Would you ever consider staying here? In Portland? We made kind of um, a good team back, there—well, I thought so. Oh, that sounds so lame, sorry."

Janelle smiled. "No. this place is *not* for me. Ever thought of moving to Florida?"

"Hmm." Henry picked up the lighter from the arm of Digger's chair. "Nope. Never have. Not until now, that is."

THIRTY-FIVE

HEAVY RAINS FALL ON and off for days, fast-moving storms that dilute the blood on the ground. This, and the recent orgy of feasting, nearly doubles the size of the Spiral, acres of new tendrils feeling their way through the earth, mice skittering, dozens of fresh voices calling out in joy, or dismay, or madness. Each one a point of silver light added to the greater whole. The Cavity too has grown, the pit deeper and wider, the beak larger and more vicious, its hunger still unsatiated.

The hapless Kolchaks are no more, but Dorothea already senses others in the forest, more outcasts in search of somewhere to rest their weary souls. For now, she has resolved to let them be, to let them proliferate and draw others, striking only when the moment is right. There are plenty to choose from—those cast out of the cities, out of society, looking for something, anything, to be a part of. A sea of meat for the taking. The Spiral will grow larger, stronger, adding new voices, until it is a city unto itself, an edifice even humanity will not be able to deny.

And Janelle... Her sister... Had that happened? Or was it just another part of this strange, unfolding dream? Why would Janelle be here, so far from home? The sense image had come through strong enough though, shocking enough, for Dorothea to recall her strike. Sentiment, or nostalgia, or...love? One of these things had pushed her to allow this ghost-Janelle a chance for survival. It didn't matter. Janelle, if it was her, would in time join the multitudes in the Spiral. The shining silver band. The insatiable collective. The escape was only temporary. Dorothea, or what was once Dorothea, is certain of it.

The soft tread of feet on the loamy floor of the forest draws her attention.

"This place is so strange." A human, his voice young, barely out of childhood. "Dude, do you feel it? The faint vibrations in the ground? Weird. What could that be?"

"I think all the vibrations are in your fool's head." An older voice. Gruff and worn. "You need to stop smoking that crater shit, or whatever it's called."

"Kratom, dude. You don't feel that? Maybe *I am* goin' crazy."

Dorothea raises a bank of tendrils, gentle feelers, their downy heads rising from the soil to stroke the men's pant legs.

"What the hell are those?" the younger asks, reaching down to run his fingers through the tufts of tender green buds. "Looks like fuzzy bean sprouts."

"I don't touch bug stuff." The older man sniffs. Dorothea smells him, piss, and rot, and chemicals. "Nature creeps me the fuck out. Give me some good, old-fashioned asphalt any day of the week."

"Oh, it's so soft. Feel it. You're crazy, dude. This is the shit we all need. Gettin' back to nature, ya know?"

The entity at the center of the Spiral pulses, *hungry,* and Dorothea feels the command like a prime directive. She wakes the silver things asleep in their Cavities, any last semblance of patience abandoned. Just as the sky releases a fresh torrent of black rain, a Cavity opens beneath each of the men's feet, and they scream, howling as the deluge washes their hot, nourishing blood into the open mouths of a hundred grasping ghosts.

END

About the Author

Marc Ruvolo (he/him) is a queer writer and musician living in Portland, Oregon who once considered himself a punk. He founded the seminal Bucket O' Blood bookstore in Chicago, and the DIY punk label Johann's Face Records. Waste ground is his third horror novella and set in his hometown where few truly know what terrors lurk beneath the surface. Find him on all the major social media platforms and say hello.

Acknowledgments

Special thanks to Joel Midden, David-Jack Fletcher of Slashic, most Portland weirdos—and of course you, dear reader.